THE JOONA TRILOGY ★ BOOK 2

Defenders of Joona

K I M V. E N G E L M A N N

NAVPRESS

BRINGING TRUTH TO LIFE

NavPress Publishing Group

P.O. Box 35001, Colorado Springs, Colorado 80935

The Navigators is an international Christian organization. Jesus Christ gave His followers the Great Commission to go and make disciples (Matthew 28:19). The aim of The Navigators is to help fulfill that commission by multiplying laborers for Christ in every nation.

NavPress is the publishing ministry of The Navigators. NavPress publications are tools to help Christians grow. Although publications alone cannot make disciples or change lives, they can help believers learn biblical discipleship, and apply what they learn to their lives and ministries.

© 1995 by Kim V. Engelmann

Library of Congress Catalog Card Number to be assigned.
ISBN 08910-98666

Cover illustration: Dan Craig

The stories and characters in this book are fictitious. Any resemblance to people living or dead is coincidental.

Printed in the United States of America

1 2 3 4 5 6 7 8 9 10 11 12 13 14 15 / 00 99 98 97 96 95

FOR A FREE CATALOG OF
NAVPRESS BOOKS & BIBLE STUDIES,
CALL 1-800-366-7788 (USA)
or 1-416-499-4615 (CANADA)

CONTENTS

Chapter   1: Laurel Returns   7

Chapter   2: Heather Meets Laurel   14

Chapter   3: The New Adventure   24

Chapter   4: Waiting for Evening   32

Chapter   5: The Takeoff   40

Chapter   6: Flying to Joona   47

Chapter   7: The Pillar of Light   54

Chapter   8: The Sacred Writings   62

Chapter   9: The Crimson Room   68

Chapter 10: Heather's Star   77

Chapter 11: The Date   84

Chapter 12: The Door in the Rock   94

Chapter 13: The Plan   99

Chapter 14: The Attack   110

Chapter 15: The Penance Room   119

Chapter 16: Sebastian   129

Chapter 17: Laurel Comes   137

Chapter 18: The Rescue   144

Chapter 19: The Restoration   151

Chapter 20: Going Home   160

CONTENTS

To my mom and dad

1
LAUREL
RETURNS

The tall, spindly trees at the edge of the river looked like quills stuck in a bed of cotton. The ground mist floated around the skinny black trunks in ghostly silence, dispensing treasures of frothy dew on the mossy bank. It was a gray dawn with a touch of chill in the air, especially when the wind gusted. To one inexperienced in shades of difference these things might have seemed fairly normal for the breaking of day in mid November.

At first, Craig noticed nothing unusual as he tramped through the soggy woods behind his sister. Why she always had to get to school forty-five minutes early he could never figure out, but his mother insisted he go with her as far as his turnoff, for safety's sake.

Craig was barely awake, and with his head down and his hands shoved deep into the pockets of his red plaid jacket, he was not in the mood for observing things anyway. All he could think about was crawling back under the covers and going to sleep. With this mindset he might not have noticed anything at all had he not stumbled as he climbed up the steps to cross the swinging bridge.

The trip-up jolted Craig wide awake. Slowly, ever so slowly,

7

he got back to his feet and began to look around. His eyes widened and his mood dramatically altered. He was suddenly aware of things being different from the ordinary. It was nothing that he saw. No. It was rather the heavy fragrance of pine and lilac that lingered in the moist morning air. There were many pine trees but no lilacs growing nearby. Still, the whole area around the swinging bridge was full of the rich scent of both. The fragrance was so intense that Craig, who kept looking all around him, insisted on staying behind.

"Go on, Heather!" he called, as his sister hesitated warily on the bridge. "I'll catch you up."

"I'm supposed to watch you, dummy!" Heather piped back. "You act as though you've seen a ghost! Better come with me or you'll be late."

"Just go on!" Craig said, motioning with a wave of his hand. He knew his sister didn't care. She just didn't want to get in trouble. "I won't tell Mom."

"Are you sure you know the way?" Heather asked absently, and then she disappeared across the bridge and into the woods without even a glance backwards.

Craig's heart pounded in his chest as he stood alone on the bridge breathing in the pine and lilac. The fragrance filled every pore of his skin with tiny, tingly vibrations. He was so excited he could hardly keep from shaking. It had been so long since he'd smelled it and he knew the alluring aroma meant only one thing—Laurel was quite near. How he had missed the swan! It was only seven months since Laurel's departure back to Joona, but not a day had gone by when he hadn't daydreamed about the swan. And the nights too were filled with colorful swan dreams where he would find himself riding high on Laurel's back, up over the world looking down, hurtling headfirst into the wind with his thin blond hair flying out in all directions. Laurel! Where was he?

Craig scanned the misty shoreline from his perch on the

bridge and at first could see nothing. The mist swirled faintly upward now like smoke from a distant chimney, wrapping itself loosely around the branches of some of the trees and disappearing into the gray morning sky. The only sound was the tireless rush of the river and the drip, drip, drip of the pine trees as the rainwater fell off them onto the soggy bank. The river seemed almost alive as it giggled and gurgled over the tops of rocks and roots just below the surface.

Then, as if shouting a bold "Surprise!" the sun, which had hidden itself well all morning, burst through a break in the clouds and made the river's surface teem with tiny flecks of rainbow. Later, Craig couldn't figure out if the swan emerged from the mist at the exact second the sun broke through the clouds or if the brilliance of the sun made the mist transparent enough so he could see Laurel strolling along the bank, his feathers shining a blinding white. Indeed, Craig couldn't look directly at the swan because of the bird's radiance. He turned away, but when he turned back again the overpowering brilliance had faded, and although Laurel was still remarkably bright, he could see the swan clearly for the first time.

It was definitely Laurel. No doubt about that. Craig felt the teeny, tingly vibrations explode inside his chest and a wonderful warmth filled him, radiating outward from his chest down his arms and legs. For a moment he just stood there unable to take his eyes off the beautiful bird. But before he could catch his breath to say anything or call out, Laurel looked up at him almost as if he had been expecting Craig. Their eyes met and the swan's neck bent down low in a swan smile. Then, raising himself to his full height, Laurel opened both his pearl-white wings in an expansive welcome.

"Craig!" the swan called with a delighted voice. "Craig! Cross over the bridge and come to me. I have been longing to see you for what has seemed like an eternity."

Craig didn't hesitate. In fact, the radiating warmth compelled him forward. He could never remember actually making it across the swinging bridge. All he could remember was that seconds later he was enfolded by the swan's rich, deep wings. He rested his head against the bird's soft chest and relaxed. He might have fallen asleep, for he had no idea how long Laurel held him. But when he awoke, if it was true that he actually did fall asleep (although it may have been a kind of trance, he wasn't sure), two things stabbed at him and made his thinking very clear. First he recognized with a jolt that his head lay right next to the chest wound his father had inflicted on the bird. Second, he found himself painfully aware of the glaring fact that he had never adequately thanked the swan for saving his life. Certainly he had been grateful; that was not the point. He just hadn't said anything to express it, and he couldn't allow the horrible truth of the thing to last a moment longer.

"Laurel," he spoke softly, so softly that the swan bent his head down low to hear him.

"Laurel," Craig said again, a little louder this time, but with a tremor.

The wound in the bird's chest, although healed and partially covered with feathers, still looked hideously deep. Craig pulled back and stood facing Laurel. The swan cocked his head and waited. The morning air was sweet with the aroma of pine and lilac, and with tiny gusts it gently blew Craig's light wispy hair back from his brow.

Craig wanted to say thank you at that moment more than he wanted to live. It welled up in him like music wells up in an organ, and yet he stood there awkwardly because he was afraid it wouldn't sound right. Instead he said something he didn't want to say.

"Will that . . . that mark on your chest . . . will it ever go away?"

Laurel looked surprised and thought a moment.

"I think it would be quite difficult for me to get rid of it as it would mean changing everything as it was meant to be."

"But won't Joona water heal it?" Craig floundered.

"One day," Laurel promised with a nod. "But not now. The time isn't right yet."

"But," Craig insisted in high-pitched fervor, "if it hadn't been for my father. If he hadn't shot his gun. . . ."

"Oh, I see." Laurel's black eyes flashed at Craig with understanding. "It is hard to look at, isn't it? It isn't the most beautiful thing in the world for you yet, I suppose."

"It must have hurt."

Laurel paused for several seconds before replying.

"You'll never know," he said softly. "Nor are you meant to know nor would I wish you to know."

The breeze gusted in Craig's face again, and the swan stood motionless, staring at him with soft, penetrating eyes that seemed to Craig to see everything that had ever happened in the world, and to him in particular.

"One day," Laurel chimed at him in the breath of the wind, "this wound will look quite different to you."

The swan bent down low in a swan smile. Craig was rather embarrassed by Laurel's accurate perception that the wound bothered him, but he loved the swan more for understanding. Again he threw his arms around Laurel's long slim neck, pressing the swan's bony cheek against his.

"Thank you," he whispered, for that was the best he could do.

Laurel nuzzled him with his beak and the sun again broke through the misty haze and encircled them in a pyramid of light.

"Take me for a ride, Laurel!" he begged, stroking the swan's back with the flat of his hand. "I've missed our rides together. I've missed Joona and the night adventures! Life is so dull, Laurel, when you have to live in just one world. I've decided it is far better to live in two and go back and forth between them."

Laurel ruffled his feathers and seemed pleased.

"You are quite right! Two worlds are better than one, as they say!"

"You mean heads," said Craig. "Two heads are better than one."

"I shouldn't think I would want more than one head!" Laurel exclaimed, startled. "I wouldn't know what I thought! Is that really what they say here?"

"Never mind," said Craig, who wasn't quite sure what the saying was really supposed to mean anyway. "It isn't important."

"Well, it is rather confusing, even if it's not important," Laurel said, ruffling his feathers a bit. "That's the downy side of living in two worlds. Sometimes you get quite a shock going from one to the next. Sometimes certain things are just impossible to understand."

"Take me to Joona," Craig begged the swan, "flying on your back like last time. Take me there, Laurel. Please!"

Laurel bent down and looked at Craig with eyes that shone like black diamonds.

"And so you shall go!" the swan breathed mysteriously into his ear. "And so we shall all go!"

The words were scarcely out of the swan's beak when there was a loud screaming, a flurry of leaves, and a crackling of brush and branches down the bank a fair distance from where they stood. Craig spun around in time to see a colorful, oblong ball roll jerkily out of the woods. Almost immediately he realized that the oblong ball was not a ball at all but two bodies locked together in fierce combat, pounding each other with fists and feet. They screamed at each other between gasps and grunts.

"You stupid jerk!" one of them yelled. "You dirty, filthy pig!"

Now the other one was on top, flailing with fists. Craig took a few steps forward. He couldn't see through the tall grass that fringed the edge of the wood well enough to make out who they were, but their voices sounded familiar.

"I've had it with you . . . you liar! You fool!"

"Oh yeah?" the other voice countered.

There was more struggle and a few groans. Then the other body was on top.

"Nobody calls me a liar without getting a full fist in their mouth and teeth down their throat!"

Craig looked around for Laurel, but he was nowhere in sight. Craig began pushing his way through the weedy grass.

"Stop! Stop it!" he called out to them. "No more! Cut it out!"

Craig thought he'd jump into the middle and break it up. No, he'd reason with them first, then try pulling them off each other. On the other hand, it might be wiser if he ran for help, but by then who knows what they might do to each other? No, it was quite clear. He would have to handle it alone somehow. He wondered where Laurel was.

When he finally reached the scene and looked down at the two writhing bodies, he recognized both girls at once.

2
HEATHER
MEETS LAUREL

Craig stood watching them for a second or two. *They were maniacs*, he thought. Completely out of control and animal-like, scratching and clawing and batting about furiously with their fists. He cleared his throat and was about to say something not very nice at all to shock the two fighters out of their combat when quite without warning a voice rang out behind him.

"Margaret!"

Craig gave a sigh of relief. It was Laurel's voice. He would know that voice anywhere.

"Margaret!" Laurel chimed out again. "Do you do well to be angry?"

The squirming bodies stopped short. A pine and lilac fragrance blew in on them. Then the air was still.

"Heather!" Laurel's voice called, penetrating the still air. "Heather! If you must wrestle someone, wrestle with me!"

"What the . . .??"

Heather Fitzgerald pulled herself up on one elbow and blinked rapidly. She had a swollen eye and a scratch across her forehead. When she saw Laurel standing near her, her eyes, even the swollen one, grew as big and as round as donuts. For Margaret, however, there was no hesitation. Something like a warm firecracker had exploded inside her when she heard the familiar voice. Quickly she scrambled to her feet. Her nose was bleeding slightly and both her braids had come undone. Laurel tilted his head sideways at her in a half-amused and half-bewildered greeting. For a split second Margaret wondered why, of all times, Laurel had chosen this particular moment to show up. It was not every day she was in a fistfight, although she had gotten into more of them than most girls her age. She so much wanted to impress Laurel, and this whole display was certainly unbecoming as far as she was concerned. None of these thoughts, however, was more than fleeting shadows once she laid her eyes on the big beautiful swan she loved. She threw herself into the swan's warm, feathery embrace. She felt the tears coming, and as they dripped down her cheeks, all she could say over and over was, "Laurel . . . Laurel . . . I've missed you so."

Laurel held her close and rocked her back and forth.

"And I missed you," the swan would say each time Margaret repeated herself. "More than you know."

Heather's eyes were still wide . . . wider than Craig had ever seen them. Her mouth was wide too. First she looked at Craig, then back up at Laurel, and slowly she began to crawl backwards on her elbows until she sat with her back plastered up against a tree, gawking at the swan.

"What the . . ." she kept whispering under her breath.

Craig walked over to his sister and squatted beside her.

"What a scene you made," he hissed. "How could you act like such an animal?"

Heather was not looking at Craig. She was not hearing him either. She stretched out her arm and pointed at the bird.

"That swan," she gasped. "It's talking!"

"That swan happens to be Laurel," Craig informed his

sister with a hint of superiority in his voice. "Laurel is a very great swan and you made a dreadful scene in front of him."

"That . . . that . . . swan is enormous!" gulped Heather in dazed amazement after a long while. "Is the thing safe?"

"Oh, you never know what I might do," Laurel piped up for the first time, looking directly at Heather with shining eyes. Margaret turned and looked at Heather too. Heather seemed quite small all of a sudden.

"Or eat for that matter," added Laurel with dignity.

It was then Laurel winked at Margaret, but Heather didn't see. The wink told Margaret that Laurel knew how it had been between Heather and her. He knew about all of her horrible days at school. He knew about the reason for the fight. It had to do with the swan himself and with Joona. Laurel knew.

Heather had not believed a word of it once she found out. She had tormented Margaret day after day in school, telling everyone that Margaret was a raving lunatic with swan's disease. It got so bad that the other kids had kept their distance from Margaret because Heather told them that if they got too close they might get invisible spots. That was how swan's disease started. It crept all over your body slowly, oh so slowly, without your knowing it, and when you were full of invisible spots your teeth fell out and your face got wrinkled like a prune. It all took about three years, Heather told them, although you could never be sure. It might hit more quickly for some.

Margaret couldn't believe how well Heather could lie. She was mortified on the playground when no one would let her play jump rope or join them for four-square. In the cafeteria she had to eat alone or with the lower grades. She didn't suppose everybody believed Heather. It was just that no one wanted to get on Heather's bad side. She wondered what fate had allowed her to be in the same class with Heather

Fitzgerald two years in a row. Ryan was in a different class at the other end of the building this year, and Craig was still in elementary school.

Not that Margaret had intentionally told Heather anything about the swan. She had not said so much as a word to anybody since her return from Joona except, of course, to Craig, Ryan, and Uncle John.

It had all started one night when she and Ryan were invited to Craig's house for s'mores. They were alone in the house by the fire, or so they thought, chatting away about Joona and Laurel. The three of them had become fast friends since their amazing adventure to Joona. It just seemed that ever since then they all understood each other in a kind of unspoken way.

Craig's parents were on an errand and Heather was supposed to be at school for play practice. Heather had gotten the lead role in the play *Oliver* because she was so good at singing "Food, Glorious Food!" far better than any of the boys who tried out. They were going to stick her long blond hair under a derby cap and teach her to speak with a Cockney accent, Heather bragged to everyone.

Margaret had just mushed her s'more together so that it was all melty and squishy when Ryan said, "I wonder how long it will take Laurel to come back. Maybe he won't ever return in our lifetime."

"He will!" Margaret assured him. "Uncle John told me that once Laurel was your friend he was always your friend. And if he is our friend, he probably misses us in the worst way right now and can't wait to come and see us again. I mean, we really want to see him, so he must really want to see us too. Of course a magic swan like Laurel can't be controlled. It would take all the fun out of it. It's far more exciting not to know when he may appear. I mean, just think! At any time, at any moment, that great big wonderful, magical swan could come swooping into the living room and scoop us all up and take us away. At any second it could happen!"

At that moment Heather walked into the room. The music teacher was ill and play practice had been canceled. She had returned home from school soundlessly and slipped into the broom closet intent on knowing what Craig, Ryan, and Margaret were talking about. The close friendship that had developed between those three puzzled her, and she hated being left out of anything.

"A magic swan, you say!" Heather had declared sarcastically, striding into the living room. "I knew you were slow, Margaret, but not loony. I hope your big feathered friend does take you away soon. It will be better for all of us."

That had been the beginning of the end. Today Margaret had decided she'd taken enough of Heather's flak. She left the house early and waited by the edge of the woods near school for Heather to appear. Heather always walked to school through the woods and she always got to school forty-five minutes early. Margaret figured she was just in time. Sure enough, within seconds Heather appeared around the bend, and when she did, Margaret jumped at her. Heather was so startled that she fled into the woods and Margaret didn't catch up with her until they reached the river.

Now, as Laurel approached Heather with his wings outstretched, Margaret could scarcely suppress her laughter.

"Being around me is actually not recommended," the swan was saying, "unless you are quite willing to live dangerously."

"I'm getting out of here!" Heather whined, scrambling to her feet. "This is too weird."

Craig grabbed his sister's sleeve.

"Don't leave until you meet him!" he insisted, trying to drag her toward the swan. "He's actually quite charming."

"Do I look real to you, Heather?" Laurel asked, still moving toward her.

"How do you know my name?" Heather demanded, shrinking back.

"He always knows everyone's name," Craig piped up, still pulling her in the opposite direction. "That's the way Laurel is."

"Are you afraid of me, Heather?" Laurel asked her solemnly.

Margaret thought Laurel looked like an angel just now, like the kind she had seen in church windows. The sun coated the swan's outstretched wings with a glaze of shimmering gold and the remaining mist on the ground made it look as if Laurel were walking on the clouds of Heaven.

"Do you . . . eat children?" Heather gasped, as the swan stopped walking and brought his head down close to her face in order to look her in the eye.

Margaret giggled and Craig clapped his hand over his mouth to stifle his own laughter.

"Children are my specialty," Laurel replied casually. "I love children."

There was a long pause as Heather and Laurel locked the other's gaze. Heather's eyes were wide with horror. Laurel's were deep and patient.

"You are meant to come with us," Laurel said finally.

"I'm not going anywhere!" Heather whined. "If you're going to eat me, then get it over with now. If not, then let me go at once."

"Not her!" Margaret begged. "Please, Laurel. Anyone else but her. She'll ruin it for all of us."

"Ruin it?" Laurel looked Heather over again quizzically. "Really?"

"I don't want her either!" Craig declared emphatically. "She's mean."

"Are you mean?" Laurel asked Heather sweetly with a light furrow in the feathers of his brow.

"No!" Heather said, stamping her foot. "I'm just not weird like they are."

"Oh!" Laurel nodded. "You mean you're of a different breed. Like the difference between a wood duck and a loon."

"I suppose so," Heather agreed warily.

"I can understand then," Laurel said, pulling back his head and glancing at Margaret and Craig. "I can understand why you wouldn't want to be included in our new adventure, especially with *them*. Birds of a different feather cannot flock together. Please feel free to leave, and my best regards to your father."

Margaret breathed a sigh of relief and settled herself cross-legged in some shorter grass near the bank. Heather would be a curse on the whole venture no matter which way you looked at it. She couldn't wait to hear what Laurel was planning for them to do. When Margaret looked up, to her dismay she saw Heather still standing by the tree awkwardly twisting her fingers together and looking at her toes. Laurel had turned his back on her and was shuffling through the grass toward Margaret.

"Excuse me!" Heather called out to the swan after a few moments had passed. "May I ask what sort of adventure you mean?"

"It wouldn't interest you, my dear girl," Laurel answered her without looking back. "It's a far too delicate matter to be handled without kid gloves, and you don't impress me as a kid at all. You seem to have grown up inside, ahead of yourself."

"But I am a kid!" Heather announced sincerely. "I'm only eleven."

"Really?" Laurel stopped and looked back at her. "I would have bet my tail feathers you were much older than that."

Margaret knew how Heather hated to be left out of anything. Certainly the swan wasn't seriously considering bringing Heather with them wherever it was they were going. Laurel knew how badly Heather had treated her. Why couldn't Heather just leave them alone instead of standing there like a complete moron?

Craig plopped down next to Margaret and rolled his eyes.

"That's all I need!" he whispered to Margaret. "My older sister tagging along like a shadow."

"Could I . . . could I come then?" Heather called to the swan.

"Suit yourself," Laurel replied mildly. "That is, if you are sure you are only eleven."

Margaret was horrified.

"Laurel!" she begged loudly, not caring if Heather heard her or not. "Please! Not Heather!"

"Margaret!" The swan looked completely taken aback. "You look so worried. There is nothing to be so concerned about. All birds change their plumage. There is a season when they molt and grow new feathers. I think it shall be so with your friend."

Margaret was about to explain that Heather was not her friend, not even in the smallest way. She was also about to protest loudly that if Heather was included in this great adventure, she was not going to go. Of course, Margaret didn't really think that was quite true. She wanted to be with Laurel more than anything in the world, and if she had to share him with her archenemy then she would do so, although very reluctantly. She wasn't going to let Heather Fitzgerald take Laurel away from her.

Margaret didn't get to say any of this, however, because just as she opened her mouth to expound on these matters there was a loud "Hullo!" from behind them. Margaret and

21

Craig turned around to see Ryan and Theodore hanging over the railing of the swinging bridge.

"Laurel!" Ryan called out. "Laurel! Gee whiz! You came back!"

The swan's neck bent down low in a smile.

"I most certainly did!" Laurel chimed back at him. "Do come down from there, Ryan, and let me get a look at you!"

Ryan dashed across the bridge, jumped the steps, and like Craig and Margaret before him, fell into the swan's warm, feathery embrace. After a few moments Laurel pulled him back and held his face between the tips of both wings.

"You look well, Ryan," Laurel exclaimed. "Very well."

"It must be the outdoors, Laurel!" Ryan said, grinning up at Theodore who had lumbered slowly after him. "Theodore's been taking me everywhere in the woods. We're a great team. He finds hurt animals and I help him cure them. I think it's preparing me well for medical school."

"Well, I'm glad to hear it," Laurel said cheerfully. "Brothers should be a good team. Greetings to you, Theodore."

Theodore grinned, nodded, and crooked his meaty thumbs underneath his overall straps. Margaret was always shocked at how big Theodore was. Ryan sat next to Laurel, but Theodore stayed standing, watching over the little troop as if he was their appointed guardian.

"Theodore brought me here," Ryan said, looking up into Laurel's dark eyes. "It's like he knew you were around this morning."

"Thank you, Theodore," Laurel acknowledged. "I can always depend on you."

Theodore tipped his tattered straw hat at the swan.

"So the giant mute is in on this too?" Heather spat out.

She was still standing under the same tree as if she were glued there.

Ryan jumped. He had not seen Heather before. "Hey,

Laurel! What's *she* doing here? Tell her to leave. I won't have her throwing insults at my brother."

Theodore grinned more broadly and waved at Heather.

"Hey, what happened to you, Margaret?" Ryan asked, really looking at her for the first time. "You've got dried blood on your lip and your hair is all undone."

"Heather and I were fighting," Margaret said drily.

Ryan looked over at Heather. "Gee whiz, did you ever get a shiner!" he yelled at her. "You're really ugly now!"

"Well, Margaret started it!" Heather came back indignantly. "She attacked me, the little brat!"

"Children, please!" Laurel interjected with urgency in his voice. "I have something very important I must tell you, and all of this banter is dangerously delaying things."

3

THE NEW
ADVENTURE

L aurel glanced at Heather.

"My dear girl!" he called, motioning to her with his wing. "Won't you please come and join us? It won't do to have you standing so far away when we are discussing such vital concerns that pertain to the very survival of things as they were meant to be."

"What?" asked Heather dumbly.

"He just told you to get your body over here and sit down," Craig interpreted bluntly.

Heather didn't move.

"Come now," Laurel insisted gently. "It's quite safe. I don't eat mean children, they are far too tough. In actuality I don't eat children at all, nor did I ever say I did. Your fears are your worst enemy. They usually are with any of us."

Heather hesitated. Then, to Margaret's dismay, she walked stiffly toward them as if someone were pushing her against her will. Finally she sat down in the grass about six feet from Laurel, a good distance from all of them.

"Now, children. I must warn you. We only have four days." Laurel's tone was low and solemn.

"What do you mean, Laurel?" Margaret pulled her jacket

up around her neck. "Four days for what?"

"To rescue Joona from the cruel pinions of the Regalia," Laurel whispered.

Heather inched up a bit so she could hear better.

"The Regalia?" Margaret gasped. "Aren't they . . . weren't they the group of swans that tortured poor Hector because he was a different color from them? Aren't they the ones who have long lists of rules and commands that stretch a pond's length?"

"The very ones," Laurel nodded solemnly. "They have attacked Joona from the northernmost flank. It has always been a vulnerable spot for Joona and we have been attacked from that angle before. It is the part of Joona that interfaces with other worlds beyond.

"Most often we are able to deter our enemies once they see the beauty of Joona and realize we are a flock of swans that dwell in peace. We don't claim to possess the waters. We enjoy them and welcome whoever would like to come, freely. This always throws our enemies for a swan dive since they come ready to fight to possess, and we tell them it is theirs already. All they must do is continually extend the same courtesy to others as we extend to them. In other words, always welcome the stranger and bring him in joyfully.

"Most of our enemies have found this agreement workable. If they do remain in Joona, they cease to be enemies and they become our friends. The Regalia is a different story. Their very philosophy is one of exclusion, punishment, and expulsion. Only the swans that are highest in the pecking order are allowed to fly, for instance. They have long wanted to take over Joona and make it into a kind of military camp. They say they want to "purify" the place from the unworthy and bring order. This is all Sebastian's doing, of course. He is a master when it comes to distortion.

"Be that as it may, they all flew in from the northernmost

flank and took us totally by surprise. You could tell they were angry by the way they flew. Up down, up down went their wings in short little jerks, as if they were marching. Swans are meant to be graceful and to take long, glorious, wing-sweeping flaps as they soar. It broke my heart to see them acting like that, so much less than what they could be. Why fly like a sparrow if you have the wingspan of a swan? It is not mine to say, of course. It is their choice."

"Then what happened?" Ryan asked impatiently.

"Well, I could tell by the line they were taking that they were headed for the castle. The castle is the headquarters of Joona, and it made perfect sense they would go there first. I sent for the fastest swan whom I knew could overtake them (it wasn't that hard since they were flapping so jerkily!). Then I immediately arranged for Margaret's mother, who as you know has her residence at the castle, to go into hiding. I also ordered the sacred parchments to go with her."

"What are the sacred parchments?" asked Craig.

"Those are the writings of Milohe," Laurel explained. "Milohe, who lives at the source of the rainbow, is the Creator of Joona itself. These parchments are his beautiful writings, but to the common eye they appear to be simply odd configurations on aged canvas. You cannot interpret their meaning unless you know the code. In them the mysteries of the ages are explained, for Milohe has never ceased to exist. Without the guidance of these parchments, Joona would have disappeared long ago."

"So who knows the code?" Margaret asked, mystified.

"I do," the swan admitted humbly. "And, of course, Milohe himself. We work together on these matters. Of course, you too will learn it soon enough."

"Go on," Ryan begged. "Tell us what is happening in Joona now."

"But one more thing," Margaret interrupted. "Is my mother safe?"

"Quite safe," the swan assured her. "She is doing very well and sends you her love. As far as Joona is concerned, the Regalia have completely overrun the castle and are standing guard around its entire perimeter. The rest of them are inside planning their next move.

"Don't think Sebastian doesn't know that four days is the absolute limit a foreign regiment can indwell the castle without destroying the nature of the way Joona was meant to be. After three days the waters of Joona will start to become contaminated with the mire of jealousy that started this whole mess in the beginning. It will seep out from under the castle walls and into the water. Jealousy is a dark green substance and it colors everything around it. The waters will cloud and the suffering swans will be oppressed terribly under their authoritarian rule. I shouldn't be surprised if they are planning something close to slavery for them all. You saw them, Margaret, how they treated Hector."

"It was awful," Margaret said, nodding vehemently.

"So what do they want with Joona, anyway?" piped Craig, wiping his nose on his sleeve.

"They want to give Joona boundaries. It has no boundaries now, but swans, like the dark swan, Sebastian, who don't understand, think that building walls and setting down hard and fast rules will preserve Joona and keep it pure. It is absolutely ridiculous, of course. Joona has been doing fine simply because it is a place where infinite possibilities stretch in every direction. I suppose the vastness of Joona scares some dubious birds who sadly feel they must be in control of whatever they participate in. The Regalia is known for that perspective. But I am confident all of you will be able to rectify the situation within a matter of days."

"Us?" Heather croaked.

"Heather," the swan spoke cordially, "it is good to hear from you."

"What do you want us to do, Laurel?" Margaret asked the swan seriously. This mission sounded a good deal harder than the last one.

"Infiltrate the castle and rid Joona from the oppression of the Regalia!"

Laurel said it loudly and then he trumpeted. The sound echoed far away into the silent morning air and sounded to Margaret like a call to war.

"Gee whiz, Laurel," Ryan stammered after the last reverberation of the trumpeting had evaporated into solemn stillness. "Why us? Why can't all the swans of Joona just band together and kick them out?"

"It's a good idea, Ryan. But one thing would hinder it. The beautiful, sleek swans that populate Joona and float in its waters were once suffering swans, and for many it was the influence of the Regalia that hurt them the most. Joona swans are so afraid of them that they would not be able to hold their own in combat. My swans need some leadership and encouragement from land-bred, intelligent creatures. In fact, just seeing you come will give them a boost. Besides, they need kids like yourselves who have a knack for attack, like you two." Here, Laurel motioned to Margaret and Heather with his wing.

"I hardly think violence is the way to resolve issues," the swan continued with a jocular ring to his voice, "but it certainly does take courage to engage in such a fervent display of head-to-head combat for the sake of preserving one's view on things. It is that kind of resolve my swans need. Otherwise, the Regalia may convince them that slavery is actually to be preferred over freedom."

"I was attacked!" Heather pouted indignantly. "I am not

someone who attacks others like a wild animal. Margaret is the barbarian. I have no knack for combat."

Heather glared at Margaret. Margaret moved closer to Laurel and pretended she didn't hear.

"Actually," Craig replied thoughtfully, "you both looked pretty beastly when you were fighting each other. Sort of like rabid rodents, squealing and scratching in the dirt."

"You shut up!" Heather ordered him severely. "You don't know anything!"

"Well," Laurel sighed patiently. "It does seem as if there is a decision to be made. As they say to the ducks during hunting season, 'Are you all game?' "

"Of course we are, Laurel," Ryan answered enthusiastically. "We'd do anything for you. You know that."

"It will not be easy," the swan warned them quietly. "But if we do it together it will be quite an adventure, I think."

"When shall we leave, Laurel?" Margaret asked him, reaching out and stroking the swan's pearl-white wings. She longed to take off with Laurel right now and soar over hills and streams and villages. She too, like Craig, had dreamed about it continually.

"Tonight," the swan told them. "As early as possible. We must go at night, and each morning as dawn is breaking I will bring you back to earth so that no one will even know you've been gone. Of course, in Joona there is no night, so you will be in the light continually when you are there."

"I can be here by nine," Margaret said, after thinking a minute. "I'm supposed to go to bed at nine, but I can easily go up early."

"My mother is working tonight," Ryan joined in. "So there's no problem really. Theodore and I will come by your house, Margaret, and get you. I found a rope ladder in the garage and I'll throw it up so you can climb down out of the window."

29

"How romantic," Heather sneered. "I swear you two have a thing going."

Margaret and Ryan ignored her. It was the only thing you could do with Heather, unless you started a fistfight.

"I can make it by nine too," Craig agreed readily. "My bedroom is in the back, right next to the outside door."

Heather rolled her eyes.

"This all sounds pretty hokey to me," she sneered. "And suppose our parents find out? We'd be in a mound of trouble, and for what I'm not sure. It all sounds too weird."

Margaret's hopes began to rise. Maybe Heather wouldn't show up after all.

"Suit yourself," Laurel told her. "This is a matter that must be handled with kid gloves and kid gloves alone. I understand how difficult it must be if you have forgotten how to play at things. If you are an adult, as you appear to be, then you mustn't risk it. It is far too dangerous."

"But I am a kid!" Heather said, beginning to object, but at that moment everyone was distracted by the piercing ring of the school bell that could be heard nearly two miles in every direction.

"Late again!" sighed Margaret. "I wonder how long detention will be this time."

"Late! I'm never late!" Heather moaned. "How could you, Margaret, you . . . you. . . ."

"It won't matter," Laurel assured them kindly. "Now all of you go and have a delightful day. I will be here waiting for you at nine. Theodore, come. Let us walk together, you and I."

Heather grabbed her book bag and took off like an arrow through the woods. Margaret placed a kiss on Laurel's smooth, feathery head.

"See you," she whispered. "Very soon."

Craig and Ryan got to their feet.

"We'll be ready, Laurel," Ryan promised the swan. "Gee whiz, it's good to see you again."

"It has done my heart well," Laurel assured him. "Very well."

Theodore tipped his hat at them as they left.

"I do think," Margaret said when they were a ways down the path, "that Theodore and Laurel must talk together somehow."

"I'm sure of it," Ryan declared. "Although I've never asked how Theodore does it. I'm not sure, but perhaps they read each others' thoughts."

"They seem to know each other really well," Craig agreed. "I'll see you all tonight!"

Craig veered off to the left toward the elementary school. Margaret and Ryan continued straight ahead.

"Why do you suppose Laurel wants Heather to come with us?" Margaret asked Ryan with a frustrated edge to her voice. "It seems so pointless."

"I haven't a clue in the world," Ryan said, shaking his head. "There's bound to be trouble with her around."

4
WAITING
FOR EVENING

When Margaret reached school, she didn't go directly to her classroom. She slipped into the girl's room and washed the blood off her face. Then she took her brush out of her book bag and braided her hair into one long, thick braid down her back because it was quicker. She noticed an ugly goose egg bump beginning to pop out on her forehead. It had a purple swirl on it.

"Stupid Heather!" she mumbled.

Stuffing her brush into her book bag, she hurried to her classroom. No teacher was present. Instead, Heather had a group of about fifteen girls gathered around her in the corner of the room, giggling. Some of the boys were standing on their desks trying to throw wads of notebook paper into the trash can. Others were playing hangman on the board. Only pale, thin Darcy Lupus, with her black horn-rimmed glasses sat at her desk studiously reading her geography textbook.

Margaret plopped down noisily at her desk, and all the girls gathered around Heather looked at her as if she had two pink antennae growing out of her head. Margaret felt particularly good after seeing Laurel and hardly noticed their stares. She couldn't wait until this evening. To go back to Joona! To see her mother again! To greet the suffering swans, Samson, Priscilla, Hector, and all the rest! To rid Joona from the evil pinions of the Regalia! To ride on Laurel's back again in the cool stillness of the night air and hear the rhythmic flap of his wings and feel the down feathers on the swan's back shuffle up around her to keep her warm!

"Margaret," a voice spoke rather coldly.

She looked up and saw Katie Babcox and Heather Fitzgerald looming above her. Katie was Heather's look-alike and best friend, except that she wasn't quite as popular as Heather because she wasn't quite as smart or as good at four-square. It was Katie who had spoken. It was the only time Margaret could ever remember Katie speaking to her. The rest of the crowd of giggling girls stood in a clump behind them.

"Margaret," Katie said again with the same icy tone, "we all think it's dreadful the way you punched Heather in the eye and attacked her by surprise. Heather would never do anything like that to you. We're all here to ask you to apologize to her or none of us will ever speak to you again."

Margaret looked at Katie with growing animosity. Yes, the two of them, Heather and Katie, were quite the pair. They both wore shiny loafers with no scratches and thin hair bands that pushed their hair back all flat and smooth on the front part of their head. Sometimes Katie's hair was a little bit messed up, but Heather's never was. It was shiny and smooth and straight. Why should Margaret care about their threats? She had absolutely nothing in common with any of them and she doubted she ever would. None of them were her friends anyway.

"I will never apologize," Margaret said in a level tone. "Not until Heather apologizes for all the lies she said about me. Heather saw Laurel today. She was with me and she knows I'm telling the truth."

"Oh that!" Heather threw up her hands in mock surprise.

"Yes, Margaret loves to play little games about talking animals. She has this swan that she insists is real and she pretends that it comes and meets her at the swinging bridge in the woods. Can you imagine? The swan's name is Laurel, according to her, and it is going to whisk her away to a magic land called Joona tonight. But I suppose if you have no friends you have to make up silly little games to amuse yourself."

The giggling behind Katie and Heather was profuse. Margaret rose to her feet in a rush of anger with her fists clenched. She would have belted Heather again had not a tall, thin man in a raincoat run into the room and clapped his hands.

"Order! Order!" he said. "Class, I am your substitute today. Mrs. Wilson is ill. Come now, everyone to your seat."

"Don't you dare come tonight," she breathed at Heather. "You come and you'll be chopped meat."

Heather glared at her.

"Oh, so you're going to attack me again, are you, you little runt? We'll see about that."

"Order!" said the tall, thin man again.

Everyone went back to their seats, and Margaret sat down slowly with her heart pounding in her chest. She should have expected it. She should expect anything when it came to Heather, but the problem was she never did, and it always caught her by surprise. Then a horrible thought occurred to her. Heather was in on it. She knew what their plans were. What if she tried to ruin the takeoff to Joona? Why had Laurel let her in on the secret to begin with? Didn't he realize Heather would be their downfall? A small, frail voice on her left whispered something and she turned quickly.

"Margaret!"

It was Darcy Lupus who sat at a diagonal behind her.

"What?" Margaret whispered back hoarsely.

34

The tall, thin man was getting himself organized and wasn't paying much attention.

"I believe you."

"Believe me? About what?"

"About the swan you said you saw. How would Heather know all the details of your imaginary game if it wasn't true? You never talk to each other. You two never even seem to look at each other much. She knew too much to be making it up on the spur of the moment. No, I believe you, Margaret. I wanted you to know. And I certainly don't believe in 'swan's disease.'"

Margaret grinned broadly and felt the anger draining out of her. Just to have one other person stick up for her was all she needed to feel good again.

"You'll have to come and see him sometime," she told Darcy softly. "He really is quite lovely."

"I will," Darcy promised. "And I'll be your friend too."

"Thanks," Margaret said with a relieved sigh. "That would be great. Would you sit with me at lunch?"

Darcy nodded and Margaret turned back to face the thin, tall man while a sense of elation welled up inside of her.

After school was over, the afternoon stretched out before Margaret like a long-division problem. Nothing seemed important to her except that she see Laurel again, and she couldn't think about much else. Perhaps she would be able to see her mother again too. That was enough in and of itself to make her spine tingle.

She and Uncle John had dinner that night. It was her turn to cook and she made chicken and mashed potatoes. Uncle John always praised her when she cooked and she liked that. It also meant that he had to do the dishes.

During dinner she had wanted to tell Uncle John about Laurel so badly, but she held her tongue just in case he would think it wasn't a good idea to climb out the window in the middle of the night. She would tell him later, after it was all over. Then he could really enjoy it all without worrying about her. Besides, Uncle John seemed to have something on his mind that evening and she didn't want to bother him.

She was just about to make her exit upstairs when her uncle cleared his throat. He was standing with his back to her at the sink, up to his elbows in soapy water, with a towel around his waist tucked in at the belt. When Uncle John cleared his throat it meant he was about to say something he'd been thinking about saying for a long time. Margaret waited, straddling a kitchen chair backwards and swinging her legs rhythmically on either side.

"What are you going to say?" she asked her uncle after she had waited a significant period of time.

Uncle John shut off the water and turned toward her, wiping his hands on the towel. He looked surprised.

"How did you know I had something to say?" he asked pointedly. "Honestly, Margaret, sometimes I think you know me better than I know myself."

"You cleared your throat," Margaret replied seriously.

"Well I was just wondering if you would mind too much if I wasn't home tomorrow evening. It would mean I wouldn't be home for dinner and then probably not for a while after that."

"Hospital rounds?"

"No. Not hospital rounds," Uncle John mumbled, and then his face sort of turned a funny reddish color.

Margaret was glad to have her uncle out of her hair tomorrow night, but he never was gone at night unless he had something going on at the hospital. He was certainly acting odd right now and she was determined to get to the bottom of it.

"Well?" she demanded. "Where will you be?"

Uncle John wiped his hands on the towel again, even though they were already dry, and sat down next to her with a worried expression on his face. John always had a worried expression on his face, but sometimes it was more worried than at other times. Right now the lines in his forehead were deep and wavy and his face was still that funny reddish color.

"Margaret," he said solemnly. "Would you mind . . . I mean would it be too upsetting for you if . . . I can always cancel out if it wouldn't be good for you right now, at this time, because I know she'll understand. . . ."

"She!" Margaret whooped. "You've got a date! I never thought the day would come! My own Uncle John is getting soft on someone! Is she pretty, Uncle John? Huh? Is she?"

John looked at his niece and smiled. When he smiled the worried lines in his face softened and waved upward.

"I'm glad you're so excited, Margaret," he grinned. "I wasn't sure how you would take it. I didn't want it to upset you."

"Upset me?" Margaret exclaimed, throwing her hands in the air. "Upset me? How could I be upset? You haven't had a date ever since I came to live with you. It's high time you started to enjoy yourself. Even Auntie Emily says you mope about too much. Before I came she said you ate out of cans all the time."

"All right," John sighed, and an expression of relief washed over his lined face. "I didn't want you to feel left out of things."

"Is she pretty?" Margaret asked again.

"Yes," said her uncle mildly. "And smart."

"Does she like kids?"

"Very much."

"When do I get to meet her?"

"Soon."

Margaret could have stayed with her uncle all night hammering him with questions. Her uncle had long ago been branded a hermit by all who knew him. He never went out to social events, and if he was invited, he often declined. She couldn't believe her ears. Perhaps a few dates would erase all the worry lines from his forehead. She wanted to know every-thing about the woman, but when she glanced at the kitchen clock, she gasped. It was 8:40. Ryan was probably waiting for her right now outside the window with his rope ladder in hand.

"Oh no!" she exclaimed. "I forgot. There's something I've just got to do. Can I go to my room?"

"Of course, Margaret," Uncle John replied. "You're sure tomorrow night is fine with you then?"

"Oh yes," Margaret reassured him. "Now don't be scared, and dress like you know what you're doing."

Uncle John laughed and tapped the top of Margaret's head as she walked by him to her room.

When Margaret got to her bedroom she ran to the window and peered down. Sure enough, Ryan was standing there look-ing up at her with a bunch of rope mounded at his feet. She screeched the window open and stuck her head out.

"Hi!" she rasped down at him. "Where's Theodore?"

"I couldn't find him," Ryan said, shrugging. "He disap-peared right after dinner. Come on, Margaret! Try to catch this thing when I throw it up to you."

Ryan took the mound of rope and tossed one end of it wildly through the air. It flew out sideways and hit the study window beneath her with a muffled thud.

"Be careful!" Margaret hissed. "Uncle John is probably in there."

Ryan gathered the rope together and tried again. This time the rope hit the bottom of her window ledge and Margaret caught it just in time by a tiny strand.

"All right," Ryan called up to her too loudly. "Attach it to something heavy like your bed."

"Shhhh!"

Margaret pulled the rope ladder into her room and

dragged it over to her bed. Then she tied both sides of the rope ladder firmly to the posts on her footboard.

"Test it!" she whispered hoarsely to Ryan.

Ryan stood on the first roped rung. Then he climbed up on the second rung and jumped a bit.

"Seems pretty sturdy," he called up again too loudly.

"Shhhhhh! Here I come then."

Margaret straddled the window ledge and then flipped onto her stomach and swung her other leg out so she was dangling with her head in the bedroom and her legs out the window behind her.

"Where is it?" she gasped. "My feet can't find the stupid rope ladder."

"Just come down a little more," Ryan urged. "The rung is right underneath you."

Margaret inched down a little bit more and felt the welcome rope ladder under her right foot. She brought her other foot down to meet it.

"Phew!" she breathed, standing up straight and still holding onto the ledge. "This isn't romantic at all. I think all the skin just rubbed off my belly."

"C'mon!" Ryan demanded. "We're going to be so late!"

"Wait!"

Margaret cocked her head. To her horror she heard Uncle John's footsteps on the stairs. Then, as she waited tensely, his steady knock rapped on her bedroom door.

"Margaret!" he called. "Are you awake? I want to come in for a minute."

5

THE
TAKEOFF

"Just a second, Uncle John," Margaret called back to him from outside the window. "I'll be right there."

"Hurry up!" Ryan hissed up at her. "He'll suspect something for sure."

Margaret pulled herself back onto the window ledge and tumbled into her room, knocking the globe off the top of her bookcase with her foot.

"Margaret? Are you okay?" Uncle John called again through the door.

"Yes. Yes, I'm fine."

Margaret rushed to the door, opened it, and slipped out into the hall to face her uncle. She couldn't let him in her room; he'd see the rope ladder.

"I just got a phone call from the hospital. They need me to go over there . . . Margaret, your face is all flushed. Are you sure you're okay?"

"I do feel rather warm," Margaret admitted weakly.

"What was all the clatter about?"

"I knocked my globe off the bookcase," Margaret confessed truthfully. She had been quite honest lately and didn't want to break her record. Her heart was pounding crazily in

40

her chest. What if Uncle John insisted on coming into her room?

"Well, I just wanted you to know I'd be gone for a while. There was a funny thud on the side of the house before. Did you hear that?"

Margaret nodded.

"Can't imagine what it was," her uncle mused. Then he paused and took one long, last look at her.

"Margaret, I want you to go right to bed. You look as if you could use a nice, long rest. I don't want you getting sick."

Margaret nodded. To her relief Uncle John was moving toward the stairs.

"See you in the morning then."

"See you," Margaret answered like a distant echo.

Uncle John disappeared down the stairs and Margaret breathed a sigh of relief. She went back into her room and locked the door behind her. Then she ran to the window.

"A narrow escape!" she rasped down to Ryan.

"Gee whiz! How did you manage that?"

"It comes with experience," Margaret replied coolly.

Again she straddled the window ledge, flipped on her stomach, and inched backwards out the window. Her feet found the rope ladder more easily this time and, after managing to close the window partway, she descended shakily to the ground.

"Finally!" Ryan exclaimed, as Margaret stood next to him brushing off the loose dirt that had rubbed off the side of the house onto her. "Now we've got to run all the way."

"Wait!" Margaret said again.

She heard the latch on the front door click.

"It's Uncle John. Quick, hide in here."

They crouched in a clump of shrubbery just in time to see Uncle John walk out the front door, get into his jeep, and roar away.

"Now," said Ryan. "Let's go!"

They darted across the lawn toward the woods as fast as their legs would carry them.

Laurel was waiting for them. So was Craig, but he didn't seem to be in good spirits. In fact, Margaret noticed as she drew near that he was pacing back and forth along the bank looking furious, his arms folded tightly across his chest. When he saw them, Craig let out a long groan.

"Finally! I thought you two would never make it! "

Laurel stood up and flapped his wings in salute. Pine and lilac wafted toward them.

"Craig is quite concerned," Laurel explained quietly, "that we take off as soon as possible. There's been a bit of a twist thrown into things, although nothing that should ruffle our feathers, if you catch my drift."

"What's happened?" demanded Margaret.

"My sister!" Craig snorted, wiping his nose on his sleeve. "As I was leaving, I heard her telling my father all about our plans. They're bound to find me if we wait a moment longer."

"The snitch!" Ryan spat out.

"I knew she'd do something hateful," Margaret sighed. "She'll probably lead them right to this spot."

"All aboard then, children!" Laurel called out. "Not a moment to lose. The time has come for a grand takeoff."

The swan held his wing out like a ramp. Craig scrambled up first. Margaret climbed up behind him, and Craig gave her a hand. The wing was slippery and the surface curved, so it was hard to get a good grip. Ryan followed.

"Hurry up!" Craig whined as Ryan lost his balance and slid halfway down the wing.

"Lights!" Margaret whispered and pointed.

Across the river at the edge of the woods, beams of yellow light made gigantic arcs across the night sky. Then they heard Heather's voice.

"Just up ahead, Dad. I promise you, you'll find him."

Ryan was struggling up the wing again.

"Grab his right hand, Margaret!" Craig said, panicking. "I'll get his left." They pulled Ryan up behind them and Margaret saw Laurel nod his approval.

Margaret had forgotten how warm Laurel's feathers were. As she snuggled down as far as she could, she felt all her chills shivering out of her in little trembles. Suddenly, as if a graceful wind had lifted them off the earth, they were airborne. Margaret could tell because Laurel's shoulder blades moved up and down like they always did when he flew them somewhere. Looking down she saw the river threading its way below them like a silver ribbon growing finer and finer as they rose up, up, and up. The reverent stillness of the night and the exhilarating motion of the swan's wings filled Margaret with ecstasy.

"Oh, Laurel!" she cried. "It's just as I remembered it, only better. You fly so well."

She looked up and saw the stars as clear as diamonds winking down at her as if they already knew the outcome of this delightful adventure. The moon was big and full and yellow. It hung low to the horizon, looking as if it had found a place of rest between two hills and was nestled there for the night. Peering over the swan's wing she could just see the tiny human lights of earth marking villages and streets. She heard a clock tolling the time somewhere beneath her, but she couldn't make it out. She felt so far away from earth, time seemed irrelevant.

Heather Fitzgerald and her dad, Casey, got to the scene just a few moments after takeoff.

"They were here," Heather muttered angrily, shining her

light around the grassy bank. "Honest they were, Dad. We're just too late. See, you can tell. The grass is flat here. Something was sitting down."

Casey stood next to his daughter and looked around. Heather was right. The grass was flat. He knelt down and felt the ground. It was warm, but it could have been a deer or any larger animal that had lain there and been frightened off by their approach. Casey was a hunter. He knew that. A gust of wind blew into his face and he sniffed the air. For a second Casey looked puzzled.

"Lilacs!" he snorted. "There's not been any lilacs in this part of the woods that I can recall."

He flashed his light around at some of the shrubbery. Nothing. To even believe in Heather's wild tale that his son was riding off on the back of a giant swan tonight was ridiculous. Granted he had seen Craig's pet swan once, standing in the road, wings outstretched like an angel, and he had kicked himself a dozen times for shooting the beautiful animal. But riding a swan was impossible. No bird, however large, could support the weight of a human being. He had been a fool to tramp out here in the night when he should be home reading his paper and drinking coffee with his wife. Casey's mouth was dry, and his throat hurt. It had been a long day out in the hot sun. Taking his flashlight over to the bank of the river, he knelt down for a drink. The water splashed up in his face and he felt something escape from his front shirt pocket and fall in.

"Blast it, Heather!" Casey fumed. "Now I've just gone and lost something in this river of yours, and I don't even know what it was. You and your stories. Craig is hiding in the house like he usually does to get attention, and I'm going to ignore it. Besides, it oughtn't to be any concern of yours. Now come on home. It's straight to bed for you."

Casey got to his feet and stomped back through the woods. Heather waited a moment before following him. Something silvery was shining at her from the branches of the brier bush on the right. Slowly she walked toward it, feeling strangely alone and sad. When she reached the bush she saw that it was a feather. She pulled it from the briers and stared at it for a moment in the glow of her flashlight. Then, to her surprise, she realized her hand that held the feather was trembling and her eyes were blurred. Heather never cried. She yelled instead. But the tears were there this evening, welling up in her eyes in droves and cascading down her cheeks.

She pressed the feather to her chest and looked up at the sky. The swan's voice pulsated in her ears. She had tried to squelch it all day by chattering incessantly to Katie, but it hadn't worked. By evening she was angry at it, and in a fit of rage at the voice's persistence, she had ratted on Craig. Now, as she stood alone on the embankment she let the voice talk to her for the first time. She didn't want to hear it really. It troubled her, but she was too emotionally exhausted to resist any longer.

"How difficult it must be," the voice of the swan was saying again and again in her mind, "if you have forgotten how to play at things. This must be handled with kid gloves and kid gloves alone. If you are an adult, as you appear to be, then you mustn't risk it."

She heard herself protesting loudly to Laurel that she was a kid. Then in her mind she heard the shrill, sharp ring of the school bell and felt the same panic rise in her throat. The swan's message overwhelmed her with a terrible sense of loss.

Gazing up at the starry night sky she remembered a time four years ago when she had spent a summer evening in bare feet on the lawn catching fireflies with Craig. She could still feel the cool grass between her toes and see the glass lanterns they had made out of empty peanut butter jars, which lined the driveway. She couldn't remember a time when she'd been happier. Then she knew. She knew more than anything that she wanted to go to Joona. She hadn't let herself feel it until now. A quiet sob escaped her. She'd had her chance, the chance of a lifetime, and had let it go like sand through a sieve. The swan would never let her back now that she'd betrayed them. Certainly they had seen the flashlights and heard her voice. Why couldn't she ever do what she really wanted to do?

"Heather!" Her father's voice was sharp and irritated. "Where are you?"

"Here!" she shouted back weakly.

Clutching her feather with tears still stinging her eyes, she stumbled through the woods toward home.

6

FLYING
TO JOONA

The swan banked to the right and Margaret recognized
their flight pattern over the Fitzgeralds' field along the
tree line. She shuddered. It was here that Laurel had
been shot. She reached out and stroked the swan's back.
Laurel bent his neck and peered back at her sideways with a
glistening eye. Craig and Ryan looked at Margaret knowingly.

"A field of memories," the swan breathed softly.

They flew on. Margaret checked her overall pocket for the
key, even though she knew it was there already. She carried
it with her everywhere. Yes, it was in her front bib pocket,
heavy and cool, lying on top of her magic feather, which also
never left her possession.

"A lovely night to soar!" Laurel exclaimed, suddenly taking
a wild dip and gliding back up again. "A pity Heather couldn't
join us."

"Laurel!" Margaret objected, catching her breath. "I'm glad
she's not with us. How can you like her, Laurel?"

The swan banked to the left and then to the right. Then he
called back to them, "Hold on!" and took a headfirst spiral dive
toward earth. Ryan clung to Margaret's arm. Craig wrapped
his arms around Laurel's neck. The spinning motion was

graceful and easy. Margaret saw the tips of the trees twirling closer and closer, but at precisely the last second Laurel swerved and soared effortlessly upward into the night sky again.

"Gee whiz!" Ryan gasped, his eyes bugging out. "I forgot how that felt. I'm still not used to it. Not used to it in the least."

"The air wants us to dance with it!" Laurel cried. "If the Regalia wasn't in Joona, I would dance all night. The air is in a perfect mood. Hardly a ripple of cross breeze."

Laurel began determinedly flapping toward the shadowy mountains. It grew darker and more breezy.

"Laurel," Ryan announced as if the swan hadn't noticed already. "Theodore wasn't around tonight."

"He is already in Joona," Laurel assured Ryan. "He has his own entrance and goes there often. Besides, he is far too heavy for me to carry with all of you."

"You mean he can go to Joona whenever he wants?" Craig asked with a whine to his voice. "Hey, that's not fair!"

"He is rather like a messenger," Laurel explained. "A human link between the two worlds. Theodore and I go back many years. He has brought many suffering swans to the safety of Joona's waters. As I am unable to come to earth often, he is my major informant as to what is going on here among the suffering swans."

They were in the mountains now, flying between two of them. It was very dark, for the moonlight was blocked. Margaret saw the river reappear way below them. It looked navy blue and murky. The swan tilted to the left and Margaret felt the pressure in her ears. They were going down. As they turned, the moonlight found them again and illuminated the ground directly below them. Margaret recognized it at once. They were descending to the mossy clearing in front of the cave door. The clearing was not large and Laurel had to fly almost straight down to avoid hitting the trees. Margaret saw the mossy green coming up to meet her and then they hit the ground with a bounce and then another bounce. Laurel ran a few paces forward and stopped just at the edge of the trees.

"Whew . . . just made it," Craig said, breathing a sigh of relief.

"Good job, Laurel!" Ryan applauded. "It's a bit harder to stop with all of us on your back, I'm sure."

"All the more fun when I have to wing it," said the swan enthusiastically. "Now children, jump down. We must make time."

Margaret jumped off Laurel's back and got her key out of her pocket. The others climbed down after her. She led the way to the rock and then into the dark, wet alcove. Water oozed from the rock here and dripped on their heads. Margaret stuck out her tongue and caught a drop of it. It made her feel tingly, light, and wonderfully healthy.

"Joona water!" she cried.

Craig got some on his hands and rubbed his face with it. Ryan let several drops fall into his open mouth.

"Nothing like it!" Craig grinned. "I'm vibrating."

"Gee whiz!" Ryan said, laughing. "Makes you want to celebrate something."

Laurel bent down low in a swan smile.

"There's plenty more inside, children."

Margaret eagerly fit the key into the lock. It went in perfectly, as she knew it would. It was not hard to turn this time either, although the lock still made a rusty, grating sound. As Margaret pushed open the door the roar of rapidly flowing water met them. It echoed off the cave walls and reminded Margaret of a choir she had once heard singing in a cathedral. She blinked a few times to adjust her eyes to the dim light of the cave. Taking a few steps forward she saw that they stood on the bank of a rushing river, which ran to the right and disappeared around the bend.

"Remember how dry it was in here?" Ryan asked, coming to stand next to Margaret.

"Yeah, and all those skeletons!" Craig shuddered.

"It's all your doing," Laurel replied. "If you hadn't opened that wall of debris built by Sebastian it would still be a desert."

"Where does the water flowing in come from?" asked Margaret, wondering if down to the left was another secret world.

"It goes underground and eventually connects to the river at the swinging bridge," Laurel explained. "The water there is actually a mingling of Joona water and earth water, although the contaminants of earth's water make the Joona water hardly recognizable. Here the water is pure."

"And clear as crystal," Margaret exclaimed. "It's beautiful!"

"C'mon!" the swan said, summoning the children with his wing. "Let's take the current to Joona. It's a billful of fun, and nearly as fast as flying."

Laurel walked down the bank and crouched in the shallow water so the children could climb onto his back. The current was swift and Laurel held his wings partway out for balance. When everyone had gotten settled, Laurel pushed off. The churning water along the sides of the river spun them around several times before they got on course. Then the current grabbed them and they were off at lightning speed, zipping through the long winding cave so fast that Margaret could scarcely catch her breath. The swan was low in the water because of the weight on his back, and tiny white-capped waves slapped the swan's sides and flew up into the children's faces. The were soaked almost as soon as they began. The water tasted sweet like honey; it was deliciously refreshing and pleasantly cool.

"I say!" Craig cried out as they whipped through the water. "My nose is clear!"

Margaret looked at him. His wet face beamed and his cheeks were ruddy. His usually pale blue eyes were sparkling at her.

"You do look different," she shouted at him over the roar of water. "You look healthier, I mean."

Ryan grinned at Margaret. His hair was soaked too, but it still stood straight up. He was licking the water off his lips.

"Sensational!" he hollered. "Sensational! It's like I've died and gone to Heaven!"

"Maybe we have!" Margaret yelled back at him.

They reached the waterfall and the quiet pool within minutes. Here the cave expanded upward and a tall waterfall cascaded down from the highest part of the cave's ceiling. Layers of water like shimmering crystal fell from the falls, one upon another, into the frothy water that led to the quiet pool. Laurel paused for a moment and the children watched the waterfall's thunderous, welcoming applause. The roar was deafening here and they couldn't talk. It seemed to Margaret as if the falls had gotten much more full and grand since their last visit. She had not remembered it being so loud. Perhaps Joona water multiplied itself once it was set free to flow.

Then they were off again, caught by the current and sailing briskly toward Joona. The walls of the cave were black and shiny like marble. Tiny waterfalls emerged at different intervals along the rocky wall and cascaded down the ridges and outcropping rocks into shining pools along the river's edge. Small green ferns had even begun to grow out of the rock in certain places, and moss had sprawled itself across some of the ledges and inlets like fuzzy carpeting.

"We must take to the sky soon," Laurel called back to them. "Remember, we aren't at liberty to land in Joona yet. You would never be able to return to earth!"

"So what?" Ryan laughed and stretched his arms up high in the air. "I love it here!"

"How can we possibly ward off the Regalia if we can't land?" Margaret asked puzzled.

"There is an exception to the rule that I'm banking on," Laurel called back to her, "although I don't usually consider it except in emergencies such as this. In fact, Theodore was granted free access and departure this way, since the well-being of the suffering swans depended upon my having a trustworthy messenger. The exception is this: In order to land we must go to Milohe. He resides at the source of the rainbow. He and he alone is able to grant us permission to land, and he will only grant permission under conditions of great need. Under these circumstances—although I can't be 100 percent certain—I can't see what would hinder Milohe from granting you land access to Joona and return passage to earth. You are quite right, Margaret. Landing is of utmost importance if we are to conquer our feathered foes."

"Gee whiz, Laurel!" said Ryan, and gave a low whistle. "Milohe sounds so very grand. Is he anything like a person?"

"Much more of a Person than you know people to be," Laurel said, "but still essentially familiar and knowable in the same manner. He is the source of all promises and expectations and the source of the rainbow itself. Now hang on, children! This is going to be a rather awkward takeoff. Much harder from the water. We are almost at the entrance of Joona."

Then, almost before he was done speaking, the swan reared backwards and began to flap his wings vehemently, sending sprays of water dancing everywhere through the air. Margaret reached out to catch a clump of Laurel's feathers for balance. Craig fell backwards against Ryan who grabbed Margaret's arm with one hand and a wad of Laurel's tail feathers behind him in the other. The three of them hung precariously while Laurel powerfully flapped, swirling the water beneath them into foamy circles. For a moment it seemed to

Margaret they were going nowhere. Then, as if a gigantic magic hand reached down and lifted them gently off the ground they were suddenly airborne. When Margaret looked up she saw they were flying directly into the rainbow.

"Welcome to Joona!" cried Laurel, as they soared into the vast symphony of color.

The children cheered, then fell silent. The surrounding beauty was too much for them to take in. The colors were not earthly colors. They were not stagnant or solid; the colors were alive and transparent. They flickered and played on the children's skin as if dancing. Whatever color of the rainbow they flew through, that was the color of their skin and everything around them. First they flew through purple, then crimson, bright green, and finally a deep gold. When they looked down, they saw the land of Joona in that same color. It was like looking at the world through tinted sunglasses or stained glass.

Margaret had forgotten how full of movement the rainbow was and how bright. The dancing colors and the brilliant light made it difficult to see Joona clearly. In fact, if she stared into the light for too long it was blinding. As they moved through the spectrum of colors, she was able to make out a small island here, a tree there, and the wide expanse of water all around. Yet, look as she might, she did not see a single swan.

"I guess they really are scared," Margaret said, leaning forward so that she could talk into Laurel's ear. "Afraid to come out of hiding. There is no lovely music this time. How dreadful! And all the swans have stopped singing."

7
THE PILLAR
OF LIGHT

"That is the whole problem in an eggshell," the swan retorted mildly. "The swans' fear of the Regalia is their worst enemy. It keeps all the lovely singing caged up inside them, and Joona music will not flow from the rainbow unless it is accompanied by their singing."

They were flying through a deep rich gold now, following the band of color as it arched into the sky.

"We will stay in the gold," Laurel told them, "until we reach Milohe. The colors shield us from being seen. When you are in the rainbow you can look down and watch, but observers looking up can only see color. This is a perfect hiding place and lookout. And only those who have been given right of passage into the rainbow can penetrate its colors as we are now doing."

"But we haven't been given right of passage," Ryan objected. "How come we're allowed in here?"

"You are with me," Laurel assured him. "And right now, I am your right of passage."

"Is it far to Milohe?" Craig asked, wondering how long of a ride they had left. He loved riding on the swan's back and didn't feel like getting off yet. The thought of confronting a host of hostile invaders was rather scary, and he was set on enjoying himself for as long as he possibly could.

"Just a little bit further," Laurel told him cheerfully. "Sit back and relax."

Margaret knew when they had reached the end of the rainbow; they all did. The aroma of pine and lilac swept up at them and the golden light faded. For a minute they were in a dense, cool cloud and could see nothing. Then Margaret felt Laurel touch down beneath her. The air cleared and a welcome breeze caressed their faces.

"This is the place," said Laurel reverently, "where all things begin and all things end. This is my home."

Carefully they climbed off the swan's back. They were standing on a stone that was completely transparent and seemed to have many dimensions to it. As Margaret looked into it, she could see that the stone was brilliant, sparkling with prisms of color as it reflected the rainbow that arched above them. The stone itself was set into the ground and was about the size of a pitcher's mound. After a few moments of staring into it, Margaret realized the stone was an enormous diamond. It was surrounded by a grassy area around which grew dark green pine trees and bushes laden with plump, purple lilacs. The aroma was far richer than any scent of it they had smelled on earth. Beyond the grassy clearing on one side where the trees parted, the water stretched out clear and shining to the horizon.

It was not any of these things, however, that captured Margaret's or the boys' attention, even though under normal circumstances they would have been awed by all of it. Rather, it was something quite unusual that riveted their eyes to the same spot. A short distance away, next to the rainbow but not part of it, stood a tall, wide pillar of light. It was up on a little knoll, and inside it there was a kind of arched, open door frame made of wood with vines hanging down from the top.

Beyond the door there was only light—white light that pulsated and moved around itself in continual uninterrupted motion. The outline of the pillar was solid and straight, however, and it stood motionless on top of the knoll. The doorway beckoned to Margaret and she took a step forward without realizing it.

"No, Margaret," Laurel cautioned. "It would mean certain death for you. You must remain here, children, on the diamond, while I go in to him. Do not worry that we have landed. This spot where we have come is unique and open for any who desire to rest. Many stop here on this diamond before moving on. It is the threshold to Milohe himself."

Laurel's face was radiant and his voice soft and tender. He began to move away from them toward the light and the open archway. As he stepped off the diamond Margaret longed to go with him. There was something deeply appealing about the doorway. She was sure she had seen it before, perhaps in a dream. She took another step forward and stopped herself when she realized her toes were at the edge of the diamond. She backed up and wedged herself in between Ryan and Craig. That way she would know if she were to move again.

Both Ryan and Craig stood motionless, staring at Laurel. As Laurel moved closer to the pillar of light his feathers took on a silvery sheen that, after a few seconds, became almost too glaringly bright to look at. When he paused to look back at them he was standing just outside the doorway. Laurel bent his neck down low to them in a swan smile. Then he took a step into the doorway. The light encircled him and he disappeared from sight almost instantly.

"Do you suppose he's all right?" Craig whispered, gaping at the open archway. "Do you suppose he wanted that to happen?"

"I'm sure it happened exactly the way he knew it would,"

Ryan responded softly, running his fingers through his pointy hair. "Gee whiz, I wonder how long it will take him to get back."

"We are to stay on this diamond no matter how long it takes," Margaret said, more to herself than to anybody else.

She looked at Ryan and Craig.

"Whatever you do, don't let me off this diamond! I keep feeling like I want to go through that door. I feel it with every part of me."

The two boys nodded.

"We probably shouldn't be looking at it," Ryan suggested. "I'm beginning to feel the same way myself."

"Then look at me, look at me!" said a tinkly voice behind them.

The three jumped and turned around. Standing on the grassy clearing in front of a clump of lilac bushes was a white swan surveying them curiously. The swan was significantly smaller than Laurel and not nearly as handsome. He had tiny yellow eyes and an orange beak. A shining metal whistle dangled around his neck.

"Welcome," said the swan, with the same tinkly tone. "You are landbred creatures, are you not?"

"Yes," said Ryan steadily. "We are."

"Are you from earth then?" asked the swan lightly.

"Do tell us your name," interjected Margaret, who was loath to give out any information to a stranger, especially when Joona was in a state of invasion. She had a suspicious feeling about this swan. He had an odd kind of stare.

"Well, forgive me!" the bird exclaimed. "How very rude of me. Actually, I don't have a name as you would call it. I have a number. It is a very nice number, however. Number 29."

Margaret and Ryan looked at each other and raised their eyebrows.

"How strange!" Craig blurted out. "Did your mother like that number when she named you?"

The swan looked irritated by Craig's bluntness, but ruffling his feathers a bit seemed to calm him. Margaret jabbed Craig in the ribs with her elbow. She didn't want to offend the creature and certainly she didn't want to see a fight begin.

"I think 29 is a very nice number indeed," she said enthusiastically. "It just suits you."

"Well thank you, my dear," said Number 29 sweetly. "I do appreciate it. My mother named me Alexander, but that is a name in the distant past. I do not use it, because it is beneath me. I have been renamed by a much higher order now. They picked out Number 29 for me, and that is what I am."

The swan was staring at them in an almost trancelike way. Although his voice was high and tinkly, it didn't seem to have much expression. He almost looked like someone's wind-up toy. Margaret pulled Ryan close to her side and whispered the word "Regalia" in his ear. Ryan nodded slightly as if he had made the same deduction.

"I dare say," Number 29 continued rhythmically, "it must be rather crowded on that . . . that stone. Why not come and join me for some berries here in the grass? Then we can chat about ourselves in a more relaxed fashion."

"We have to stay here!" Craig belted out. "Until Laurel gets back."

Number 29 jumped at the sound of Laurel's name almost as if someone had knocked into him. Margaret jabbed Craig again.

"Don't say another word!" she whispered hoarsely at him. "I'm almost sure this swan is with the enemy."

Craig's eyes grew large and he swallowed loudly.

"So then," continued Number 29, "you landbred creatures are having an outing with . . . with . . . yes with . . . another swan I know. How very pleasant! It is a lovely day to be out and about."

"Yes, it is," Ryan agreed coolly.

"So how long do you children intend to stay on that ridiculous little rock?" Number 29 asked mockingly and laughed a tinkly little laugh. "You can't possibly think your friend will return if he disappeared through that archway. No one goes in there. You can't survive it. Perhaps your friend didn't realize. . . ."

"He realized," Margaret interjected. "And we will wait here forever if we have to."

"I see," said Number 29 and sniffed indignantly. "Completely loyal to a bunch of hocus-pocus nonsense and a swan who just destroyed himself. Suit yourself. I will indulge in these luscious strawberries alone then."

Craig was pulling at Margaret's sleeve.

"How do you know he's an enemy?" he whispered. "I'm starved. I could go for some of those berries right now. My stomach is growling."

"Sit down!" Margaret ordered, and the three of them sat. "Now link arms!"

They did.

"No one leaves this diamond," Margaret hissed adamantly, "unless the other two go. I'm not going, so that means no one is going."

"I'm not budging either," said Ryan.

Craig sighed.

"I suppose you're right," he conceded. "It's just that I'm starved."

Number 29 had his head buried in the grass. When he looked up, he had strawberry juice dripping out of his beak.

"Delicious berries," he mumbled at them with his mouth full.

"We're glad you're enjoying them," Ryan said pleasantly. "As for me, I don't care much for strawberries."

"Perhaps some human food of another sort would be

more appropriate for you," sounded a familiar voice on the other side of the rock.

They turned and saw Laurel emerging from the doorway. He was walking toward them with his head held high. His whole body was a brilliant, shining white. There was a sparkle to his eyes and a spring to his step that made him seem full of boundless energy and enthusiasm. On his back was tied a blue bundle, and over one wing he carried four silver stars on chains. The other wing carried something bulky and long underneath it, but Margaret couldn't make out what it was.

"Wow!" Craig said and whistled. "You're back in no time at all. I thought it would take forever!"

"You look wonderfully refreshed, Laurel," Margaret remarked as Laurel joined them on the diamond.

She patted his gleaming white head.

"It is always so good to go home," Laurel said thoughtfully. "These worlds become such tiresome places at times."

"Pretty short visit," Ryan observed. "For your sake I wish you could have stayed longer."

"Actually, I was there for a good deal longer than it appeared to you out here," Laurel declared. "Time has nothing to say about anything once you proceed through that archway. And children! I have great news! Milohe has greeted you all warmly and granted you your right of passage as long as you wear these stars around your neck. Now listen carefully.

"These stars are made of silver, and though a bit cumbersome at times, you must never remove them. Put them on now. By wearing them you are now able to walk freely in Joona and return and depart as you wish. The only danger is that you must be careful you do not end up going to the wrong places, for these stars will allow you entrance anywhere, even into Sebastian's secret underworld. Only go where I lead you. The stars have another secret you will soon discover. I was given four. The bundle on my back is an array of delightful delicacies prepared just for you and . . . why, Alexander! Whatever are you doing here?"

Laurel had just noticed Number 29, who was trying to make a stealthy getaway into the trees. Number 29 looked taken aback and took a few more steps backwards, but Laurel was already marching toward him.

"The name is Number 29," said Alexander stiffly.

"You can't be one of them, Alexander!" Laurel addressed the swan firmly. "You're not yourself, Alexander. Your voice sounds different. Here, let me touch you."

"If you proceed any closer," Number 29 said defiantly, "I shall be forced to blow my whistle and the whole army of the Regalia will be here to arrest you within a wing's flap."

"Alexander!" Laurel's voice was definitive and commanding. "You and I were bosom friends. I am not going to let them have you."

Laurel slowed his pace but continued to walk toward his friend. Number 29 looked scared and confused and Margaret thought he was going to raise his whistle.

"Don't you remember all the fun we had together, Alexander?" Laurel spoke softly to him. "The freedom of the wind under our wings and the breeze in our faces. The stories we told and the meals we shared. I dare say it looks as though they have clipped your wings."

Laurel was quite near Alexander now. Alexander glanced about furtively with a wild look in his eyes as if he were an animal trapped in a tiny cage. In a desperate attempt to free himself he raised the whistle to his beak.

8

THE
SACRED
WRITINGS

L aurel was not in the least bit shaken.

"Don't do this to yourself, Alexander," Laurel continued in a clear, stern voice. "You are too strong for this nonsense, Alexander. I know you. Let me touch you, Alexander. Let me touch you."

Laurel reached out his enormous radiant wing and brushed the top of Alexander's head with his feathers. The whistle fell from Alexander's beak, and he crumpled to the ground and began to sob. Margaret had never heard a swan cry before. It sounded much like human crying but a bit more muffled and choppy. Laurel stood over his friend consoling him softly.

"They'll kill me for this, you know," Alexander blubbered through his tears. "I was told to keep watch here and that if I ever saw you or a landbred creature I was to lure them off the diamond and blow my whistle. That's what I was supposed to do, and now they'll kill me."

"Your voice sounds normal again, Alexander," Laurel said softly. "Rich and deep. It is good to have you back, dear friend. No one will kill you. I will protect you. In fact, you may be of great service to us just now."

"They're horrible, Laurel," Alexander said, continuing to weep. "You have no idea how they treat us. They make us into robots, Laurel—feather brains! They train our minds to think in only one way. Then they clip our wings to keep us grounded. Only the leadership may fly."

"How dreadful!" Margaret exclaimed.

"Come now, Alexander," Laurel said calmly. "Let us all have something to eat. It will refresh you. Then you can begin to chart your course against the Regalia. Children! Do you have your stars on? Good! Then come off the diamond and untie this bundle on my back. It is full of delightful, landbred food and seaweed. Alexander, please get rid of that ridiculous whistle."

After they finished eating Craig lay back and propped himself up on his right elbow. He was full. The treats Laurel had brought back for them far exceeded his expectation. They had eaten fruit tarts made of peaches and strawberries and pound cake, smoked sausage and cheese with bacon on toast, warm asparagus wrapped in a layer of melted cream cheese and fried dough, noodles in a rich cream sauce with tiny sweet peas, and finally, soft gingerbread squares. There had been a sweet, mild punch that came out of a tall dark green bottle with a cork. It was fizzy and pink. No matter how much they poured there was always more for everyone. Look as she might, Margaret could not see through the dark glass to tell how much was left, so finally she just gave up.

"Now," began Laurel, "I must leave you in a few moments. I heard from Milohe that Theodore is beside himself trying to round up the swans who are in hiding. They simply will not cooperate. What we need them to do is to band together, but they are far too afraid to be seen. I must go to them and rid them of their fears. Nevertheless," and here Laurel drew out what he had been hiding under his wing ever since he had emerged from the pillar of light, "you are to read this and do what it says. The writing is in code, and it is up to you to find the meaning. These are the sacred writings, and in them is everything you will need to know about how to conquer the Regalia. I have no doubt you will find them quite enchanting."

Margaret watched as Laurel set a short, thick scroll on the ground at her feet. It had wooden handles and a leather buckle that held it together. The scroll looked ancient. It was yellowed at the top and bottom edges, and the parchment was wrinkly.

"But . . ." Margaret stammered. "Must you leave, Laurel? I thought you could help us decode . . . I thought you knew all secrets."

Laurel paused and flexed his wings slightly as if preparing for takeoff.

"Everyone must find the secret for decoding them on their own," he said, looking at each of the children in turn and finally at Alexander. "The sacred writings would have no meaning for you if someone else was their interpreter. All of you must find the way to understand them, and when you do everything will become clear. Alexander will stay with you and assist. A swan's logic is helpful in these matters."

"Gee whiz, Laurel," Ryan commented, furrowing his brow. "What if we can't do it?"

"You *shall* do it!" Laurel exclaimed. "The future of Joona's freedom rests on your shoulders. I would not leave a matter of such great importance in the hands of incompetence. I have every faith in you. Now Alexander, children, I suggest you all move to the diamond where you will be safe from the hostilities that surround us. I must be off at once!"

Laurel spread his wings and calmly took off toward the distant horizon where the sea met the sky in a blending of blues. They watched him rise and soar until he disappeared into the crimson band of the rainbow.

"I suppose we ought to pack up our picnic things,"

Margaret suggested, feeling quite alone and responsible without Laurel at her side. "We don't want to leave the Regalia any clues as to our whereabouts."

They bundled everything into the blue tablecloth and made their way to the diamond. Alexander waddled next to them, and Margaret noticed him shaking his head back and forth rather forcefully.

"I must say," he remarked as they all got settled on the diamond, "it is a relief to be back in one's right mind again. I can't fathom where I put it, my mind, that is."

"You sure look happier," Ryan said, grinning at him.

Alexander looked much more like a cute swan now than an odd one. His eyes were brightly inquisitive and his orange beak had a crooked smile to it when it was closed all the way.

"Well," Margaret said importantly, "I suppose we ought to get down to business."

She took the scroll and unbuckled the leather straps.

"Here," she said giving one end to Craig, "you unroll it from your side."

The parchment made a crinkly noise as they spread it across the stone. There were bubbled-up places that looked like the paper had gotten wet. Tiny cracks and wrinkles covered the surface. Margaret and Craig kept unrolling until they were at opposite ends of the diamond.

"There's still a good deal more to unroll on my end," Craig shouted.

"Shhhhh!" Margaret commanded. It seemed as if she were always telling Craig to be quiet. "Just stop there. Ryan, see if you can read it."

Ryan bent over the scroll and studied it closely.

"There's definite writing here," he said, after examining it carefully for a few minutes. "It's written in all different colors with upside-down exclamation points and tiny boxes with lines cutting through them from all angles and directions.

There are dots and circles and some squiggly things that look like worms."

"Well?" Margaret persisted. "What does it say?"

Ryan looked up at Margaret and shrugged.

"Gee whiz, Margaret! What do you think I am? A magician?"

"Perhaps it's in swan language," Margaret suggested hopefully. "Give it a try, Alcxander."

Alexander waddled over to the parchment and bent his long neck over the scroll. For a moment it seemed as if he might be making some sense out of it. They waited expectantly, but when Alexander raised his eyes to meet hers, Margaret's heart sank.

"I am afraid," Alexander sighed despairingly, "that I have no more insight into these matters than you. This looks terribly complicated and I cannot make bill or feather sense of it. I have never seen such squarish script before."

"It's certainly ancient," Ryan said, looking down at the writing again. "Just about the oldest thing I've ever seen."

"Maybe if we roll out more," Craig suggested, still rather loudly, "maybe there will be a message for us further in."

"Okay," Margaret agreed. "You roll it out and I'll take it up on my end."

At first it was difficult work. Sometimes the scroll would buckle and look as though it were about ready to crack in half as they unrolled it. Finally Margaret and Craig decided to come closer together so less of the scroll was visible at any one time. It made it much easier to roll. Each time a new section appeared Ryan and Alexander would study it. Each time they would shake their heads and Margaret and Craig would have to unroll some more. It seemed to be the same kind of odd script over and over again with no change. Every other character was written in a different color but there was no regular spacing between the lines or the clusters of symbols.

"I don't know what Laurel was expecting us to do with this," Craig whined as they got close to the end of the roll. "What are we gonna do?"

"Gee whiz, maybe we're not as smart as he thought we were," Ryan sighed. "Or maybe we're not trying hard enough."

"There's got to be a way to read this!" Margaret insisted. "We're not thinking right."

Just then there was a clamor of voices coming from behind a cluster of pine trees. A voice bellowed loudly, "Number 29 was posted just about here. We'll examine him and see if he has any news for us."

"It's Number 28!" Alexander gasped with a look of desperation leaping into his eyes. "He's my immediate supervisor. If he sees me here with you he'll trap me, and if I step down from this diamond he'll have all my feathers plucked out for betraying the Regalia. I've got to hide!"

"Where?" Ryan asked, looking around helplessly. "The diamond is the only place where you're safe. They can't attack you here."

"But they'll see me and surround me and I'll starve here!" Alexander rasped. "We'll never get them to back off, just the four of us! We've all got to hide if we want to save ourselves. Quickly!"

Margaret looked around trying to find some way of hiding on the diamond, but it seemed futile. The voices of the Regalia were getting louder. She could hear them crashing about in the brush, and she knew that if they didn't do something quickly they would be discovered. She was just about to suggest they make a run for it behind the lilac bushes and take their chances at being found by the Regalia when Craig pointed to the rainbow and cried, "Look!"

9

THE CRIMSON ROOM

What they saw made their mouths drop open in amazement. Even Alexander opened his beak slightly. Descending toward them, from the crimson band in the rainbow, was a broad circular staircase with a wide banister up one side. Each step was a different color from the one before it. The steps hardly looked sturdy enough for the children to stand on, for they appeared to be made out of the same kind of misty vapor as the clouds. The staircase seemed to be unfolding as it descended out of the sky, and the colors of the stairs in sequence paralleled the colors in the bands of the rainbow—purple, crimson, green, and gold. As the last step unfurled onto the surface of the diamond they heard Number 30 calling from behind them.

"Corporal Number 29!" the burly voice bellowed. "We are looking for you. Report at once or you will be chastised for insubordination!"

Two short, shrill whistles and then a long one pierced the air.

"It's my whistle combination!" Alexander told Margaret with a trembling voice. "Any swan that refuses to respond to their whistle combination goes into solitary confinement for six days."

"They've got more punishments than they know what to do with," Margaret hissed back at him. "Hurry up, Alexander! We've got to try this staircase."

"I find it very difficult to climb stairs," Alexander told her glumly. "My legs are rather short and spread too far apart. It's best if you just leave me here to die."

"Go on, Craig," Margaret whispered, handing him the scroll that was still open. "See if it will hold you. And don't let go of that scroll whatever you do."

Craig put his foot on the first step. It was a purple step and the surface of it looked like steamy soup. His foot sank down a little but to his delight he found it solid about an inch into the color. Tucking the scroll under his arm he grabbed the railing, which he also found solid a little way in, and began to climb quickly.

"What if I fall through when I get to the top?" he called back. "Why did I have to go first anyway?"

"Shhhhhhh!" said both Margaret and Ryan together.

"We're going to have to carry Alexander," Margaret told Ryan softly. "He doesn't climb stairs. His legs are too short."

"A pity my wings are clipped," Alexander said dolefully. "I could save you the trouble."

"Link arms!" Ryan said. "And hurry! I can see them coming through the trees now. A whole band of them."

Margaret and Ryan made a seat by grabbing each other's right forearm and their own left one. Then they brought the seat low to the ground so that Alexander could waddle up on it and nestle down with his legs dangling through. When all was secure, they lifted the swan and moved slowly toward the staircase. Ryan began to climb the stairs backwards and Margaret followed going forwards with the swan in between. Alexander was heavy, and they had to pause after each step to catch their breath. The time seemed interminable and Margaret was sure they would be spotted. She looked up and saw that Craig had already disappeared into the crimson.

Sometimes, because she could not hold on to the banister, she felt as if she were losing her balance. Once she stumbled over a step but held on firmly to Ryan's forearm and recovered. Finally, exhausted and perspiring, they too reached the crimson band. The last thing Margaret heard before they disappeared into the rainbow was a voice from one of the Regalia. It was a high-pitched nervous voice this time.

"Captain! Captain! I've found Number 29's whistle. Over here, Captain, under this tree."

"Traitor!" bellowed the burly voice. "He shall die! A bosom friend of our Enemy should never have been allowed to join our faithful chosen!"

"I much appreciate the lift," Alexander said gratefully as the three of them collapsed into the crimson band. "Perhaps I will have the honor of giving you a lift one day."

"I never realized the color of this band was solid," Ryan said, looking about.

"It looks as though part of it is and part of it isn't," Margaret observed after a moment's pause. "Otherwise we wouldn't have been able to fly through it."

As they looked about they found they were in a good-sized room enclosed with glass on four sides with an opening for the staircase on one end. There was an arched window on the opposite wall that was latched shut. The ceiling was also glass and the floor was covered with a braided red rug. The only furniture in the room was a round glass table with four wicker chairs and an old lamp in a corner on a lampstand with a metal pull cord. Craig was sitting at the table staring down at something and hardly seemed to notice their arrival. The room looked out on all sides and the light streamed into the room through the glass walls making everything crimson, even the children's skin and Alexander's feathers.

"The staircase!" Ryan gasped, looking behind them. "It's disappearing!"

Indeed it was. As they watched, the colorful steps were becoming lighter as if they were dissolving. Finally they faded completely just as skywriting from an airplane fades against the blueness of the sky.

"We are perfectly safe here from intruders," Alexander said, giving a relieved sigh. "No one on the outside looking in can see through the color, but we, quite fortunately, can look out on them and see everything quite clearly."

"Thank goodness the Regalia didn't spot us climbing up!" Margaret exclaimed.

"All in the plan," Alexander said, nodding reassuringly.

"Hey, Craig!" Ryan called, getting to his feet and walking over to the glass table. "What are you looking at?"

"I don't know why you were having such a hard time reading this," Craig commented blandly, showing him the scroll. "It's perfectly obvious right here in red and white."

Ryan looked down at the scroll for a moment and then jumped back startled.

"Gee whiz, Craig! Hey, Margaret! Alexander! Get over here quick! The words on the scroll! They're ... why, they're readable in this light! They make sense!"

Margaret and Alexander raced over to Craig's side. It was true. The crimson light shining in on the scroll from all angles had transformed the parchment into a readable document. With the scroll now a deep red from the light, new words had formed to take the place of the squares and slashes that had been there before. The words were written in black script and formed two columns on either side of the section Craig had open before him.

Margaret began to read the message out loud slowly and

carefully so that nothing was missed. A certain awe filled her
chest as she read, because she realized she was saying far
more than she understood.

> To the seekers of truth desired beyond all else, and
> the lovers of justice, this information is dispensed,
> not without sacrifice, but with certain joy that the
> recipients will receive it gladly and carry out its
> meaning eagerly. You who read are located in the
> look-out room where only the followers of Laurel find
> themselves privileged to go. It is here and only here
> where you can read the scroll and undertake its
> meaning and gain a vision from the window of what
> is taking place below. This window reveals all and
> should greatly assist you in your plans. Another
> great assist for you, lovers of justice, is the latch door
> halfway up the left pillar of the castle wall. It is a
> secret door always left unlocked for emergencies and
> hidden in the rock. The enemy has not discovered
> this yet and has left it unguarded, giving you a
> means of entry if you so desire.
>
> Those leaders of justice who wish to work for the
> cause of the suffering swans must also be armed
> with distinct weapons from Milohe. The silver stars
> of Joona are your weapons. Use them confidently.
> The means for counterattack are not simple and
> must involve a community of dedicated followers of
> Laurel. A strong resistance must take place among
> many, along with a group resolve not to see things in
> the manner in which the Enemy wishes them to be
> seen. If the resistance is bold enough, and the
> resolve in each heart strong enough, then the Enemy
> will be thwarted and blinded.
>
> Finally, a last word about the convert in your

*midst. You must allow him to use his wings. Lovers
of justice and seekers of truth, go in peace and may
Laurel guide you in your mission.*

No one spoke for a long time after Margaret finished. A
reverent stillness filled the room. Margaret knew she didn't
understand all of the message. None of them did. However,
one thing in her mind was quite clear. They were involved in
a far bigger cause than she had up to this point realized, and
it left her reeling.

She wondered if the scroll had been written just for them
or if it was something referred to by ancient swans long ago
to help them in their battle plans. The reference at the end to
the "convert" in their midst using his wings could only be
Alexander. Still, she wondered if perhaps others before them
had also needed that same message in order to use their
wings effectively. She had the sudden awareness that it actually didn't matter if the message on the scroll had been written just for them at this particular time and place or whether
it had existed light-years before them, for others as well. The
point was that the message was for them, at this moment.

There could be no denying they had been led to this place
to discover the message by Milohe. The message honored
them and Margaret was taken by its strength. She had never
thought of herself before as a lover of justice or a seeker of
truth, but she supposed that if you came right down to it she
was. She certainly didn't want the swans to suffer, and she
was trying valiantly not to lie any more. As for the bit about
the window and the secret door in the pillar of the castle wall,
she was intrigued and excited.

"Is there any more?" she finally asked cautiously, breaking a silence of at least three minutes. "We wouldn't want to
miss anything."

Craig rustled loudly through the scroll for a few moments and then shook his head.

"Nope, the rest is all in squiggles and squares. It won't come clear."

"We read the part we were supposed to read," Alexander told them wisely. "The rest has not yet been revealed to us."

"Perhaps, Alexander," suggested Ryan, "you should unfold your wings."

Alexander seemed surprised, but with sudden eagerness he complied. As he spread his wings everyone could see they were wide, long, and full again. Margaret had to blink back her tears, for Alexander looked so pleased. He kept gazing at his wings, first his right one and then his left, inspecting them carefully to make sure there wasn't one feather missing.

"I dare say, I do feel like a true swan again!" he cheered happily. "These wings are as good as new, and I didn't even feel a twinge of a growing pain."

He stood up and flapped lustily at them.

"There's magic in the scroll," Margaret said to Ryan. "An ancient wise magic."

"I know," he told her solemnly. "A queer sensation came over me when you were reading. Sort of like you were casting a spell, but a good spell. That's why I told Alexander to open his wings. I had this awesome feeling they had grown back."

"Hey! I want to check out this window!" Craig demanded. "The scroll says you can see anything from here. I wonder if I can see my house!"

He dragged a chair underneath the window and promptly stood on it but still wasn't quite tall enough to reach the latch at the top.

"I expect you *could* see anything from the window," Alexander said thoughtfully, "but you'll probably see only what you're meant to see."

Margaret brought a chair next to Craig's, stood on it, and

flipped the latch. Then she pushed the window open wide. At first there was nothing but crimson light and a cool breeze wafting in on them. Then, out of nowhere, a white screen unrolled in the crimson sky, much like the ones they had all seen at cinemas. As they watched, small moving objects at the bottom of the screen appeared, looking rather like ants. The tiny creatures slowly grew larger. It looked as if a camera were zooming in on them as they took up more and more space on the screen. As the creatures grew, Margaret thought that perhaps they were mice, then she thought they must be pigeons.

The creatures struggled forward jerkily and looked as if they were carrying something too heavy for them to manage. As they continued to become more distinct, Margaret cried out with her heart in her throat, "They're swans!" It was quite clear moments later that the creatures were indeed swans. What also became clear were the castle walls in the background.

"Gee whiz," Ryan said slowly, "I guess we're getting a sneak look at what's going on in the castle right now."

The swans continued to come into sharper focus. They were thin, scrawny birds with patchy feathers and dour expressions. Their eyes were dull and lifeless and their feathers drooped. On their backs they carried large rocks, sometimes as many as five or six bundled together with rope and tied around their bellies.

"Ah yes. It's the Penance Room," Alexander told them gravely. "This is where the disobedient and the rejected ones come. They are told that the only way they can keep themselves from going to hell when they die is to continually do hard labor. The other swans tease them so and peck at their eyes until some of them from sheer exhaustion just lie down and die—hell or no hell."

"Why are they carrying such heavy stones?" asked Craig with horror.

"For the boundaries the Regalia insists it will build all around Joona," Alexander said. "They are to pile the stones outside the castle and then take them to the appointed places to eventually build a wall miles and miles high all around Joona to preserve it. The walls will only allow certain chosen ones in and keep all others out."

The swans continued to march before them across the screen in melancholy procession. Then Margaret cried out again.

"Look, Ryan! Craig! It's Samson and Priscilla! The swans we rode the night Laurel got shot. Look at them! They're barely alive!"

10
HEATHER'S STAR

"I think you're right, Margaret," Ryan agreed. "Although I can hardly recognize them. It certainly looks as if they're not going to make it much longer."

The two swans breathed heavily under their load and were pausing for ages between each step. Priscilla's left wing dragged on the ground. It looked as if it had been broken. Samson's eyes were half-shut and there was a big patch of raw, pink skin exposed on his right side.

"Landing sakes!" Alexander exclaimed, astonished. "They've plucked his feathers and broken her wing. Those two must have been real trouble for the Regalia."

"We've got to do something!" Margaret exclaimed. "Before it's too late! Those are my friends out there."

"I can't believe I was part of this foul organization," Alexander moaned. "It makes me feel mighty ashamed of myself."

"But you didn't know," Craig said, trying to be comforting. "They had you hypnotized."

"What are we going to do?" Margaret asked in desperation, wringing her hands.

"Do about what?" came a voice as clear as a bell from behind them.

Looking around they saw Laurel standing in the open doorway of the crimson room with his head bent down low in a swan smile.

"Oh Laurel!" Margaret cried, running toward him. "Oh Laurel, you've just got to help us."

She couldn't contain her grief at seeing Samson and Priscilla any longer. Wrapping her arms around the swan's neck she buried her face in his feathers and began to sob uncontrollably.

"There, there, Margaret," Laurel crooned to her soothingly, wrapping his big, fluffy wing around her. "Whatever is the matter, my dear?"

"We were looking through the window," Ryan explained sadly.

The screen had faded as soon as Laurel spoke to them and now only crimson light and a cool breeze swept through the open window.

"You broke the code then," Laurel said softly. "I knew you would. Good job."

"Yes," Ryan admitted. "But when we did look through the window we saw Samson and Priscilla in a horrible state."

"Wings broken and feathers plucked," Alexander said, shaking his head.

"And they're carrying a bunch of big rocks on their backs too," Craig added solemnly.

Laurel's face looked stern.

"I can see now that we don't have a moment to lose," he said firmly. "There can be no delay. Theodore and I have prepared the swans who are in hiding as best we can. I was hoping for a little more time with them to rev up their spirits, for they are still rather frightened, but I can see now that we cannot wait. The swans in hiding are willing to assist you, children, and we must trust them to give what they can. Tomorrow we shall infiltrate the castle according to plan."

"Tomorrow!" Margaret managed hoarsely, lifting her head up off Laurel and wiping her eyes. "We can't wait until tomorrow! Samson and Priscilla need us now."

"Dear Margaret," Laurel assured her with deep compassion in his voice, "I know just how you feel. But I must take you home now. Morning is breaking on earth where you live. I shall see you in the evening, and then we shall rescue Samson and Priscilla from the cruel pinions of the Regalia, and all the others who are in bondage with them. Come now, children! Up on my back and we will take to the air. You are all tired and I hope you will sleep on the journey home. Oh, one other thing, Margaret. Here, this is for Heather. Do give it to her for me and tell her she is still welcome."

Laurel brought out the fourth silver star from under his wing and handed it to Margaret who reluctantly placed it around her neck with the other one. She had suspected the fourth silver star was for Heather but hoped she was mistaken. She didn't know why Laurel kept pursuing this thing with Heather, but she was too tired to protest. Wearily Margaret climbed up the swan's wing and sank into the down. She felt Ryan and Craig settling in beside her but she was asleep before Laurel even left the floor.

The next thing Margaret remembered was waking up in her own room quite refreshed. The rope ladder was still tied to the bed and the window was open. She thought of Samson and Priscilla and shuddered. Then she saw the two silver stars hanging around her neck. She had half a mind to throw Heather's in the wastebasket and tell Laurel she had lost it. It might keep Heather from joining them that night, if she intended to come at all. Besides, she was convinced that Laurel didn't understand quite how mean and double-crossing Heather could be. Then she remembered the scroll. She had never thought of herself as a seeker of truth. If that was what she was, then she mustn't lie, she thought reluctantly. Sulkily she tucked both stars into the front bib pocket of her overalls as she got dressed, and zipped it shut. Heather was a hopeless case, but she would give her the star for Laurel.

Margaret's teacher, Mrs. Wilson, was still sick that morning, and the tall, thin man came back in again to teach. He was nice but couldn't seem to keep control of the class. When he talked, everybody else talked too in low murmurs all around the room. When he turned his back to write something on the chalkboard some of the boys would shoot rubber bands into the wastebasket and tip way back in their chairs. Once, during science class when the tall, thin man was talking about astronauts, Clyde Thompson slipped and fell backwards in his chair with a big crash. Clyde wasn't hurt and everyone laughed, but the tall, thin man was nervous and sent him to the nurse. Clyde didn't come back for three hours and told everyone later that he'd gone to the store and bought grape twizzlers.

Margaret watched him selling the twizzlers on the playground for an enormous sum after lunch that afternoon. She and Darcy were on the swings talking about it. Clyde had a crowd of kids around him; although Margaret and Darcy both loved grape twizzlers, neither of them had any money, and even if they had they both agreed they wouldn't dream of giving it to Clyde Thompson.

Darcy had to go in then to do a make-up quiz and Margaret was left alone. She had been extremely grateful for Darcy's friendship over the past two days. It felt good not to be alone all the time at school. It made her feel less odd. She hadn't shared anything more with Darcy about Laurel. Margaret supposed Darcy understood that Laurel was the kind of secret you just couldn't talk about casually with anyone at any time. So far, Darcy seemed to understand that.

She fingered the silver stars through her denim pocket. They were heavy and Margaret had been aware of them all morning. She had waited for an opportunity to give one to Heather, but Heather had appeared sulky all day and out of sorts. She hadn't walked by Margaret's desk once. Usually she was popping around the room all the time, running up to talk with the teacher, asking permission to go to the bathroom to comb her hair, volunteering to erase the board, and "ooohing" and "ahhhhing" when she raised her hand with the right answer, which was all the time. Today Margaret had hardly noticed her. She sat sullenly at her desk, and if any of her friends stopped by to chat she shooed them away with a scowl.

"I guess she doesn't feel well," Margaret heard Katie tell another girl in the lunch line. "Just ignore her. She'll probably feel better tomorrow. Besides, who knows? Maybe she got a bad grade or something."

Margaret sighed. Of all days for Heather to be out of sorts. She certainly wouldn't want the silver star now. In fact, she'd probably smack Margaret right across the face and they'd have another brawl right in the middle of the playground. Nevertheless, Margaret had resigned herself to follow Laurel's wish.

She scanned the playground trying to find Heather. When she found her she would simply go up to her, hand her the star, and say, "Here. This is from Laurel to you." That is all she would say. Then, if Heather didn't ask any questions, she would turn and walk away. If Heather smacked her, then she would smack Heather back. If Heather didn't want it, she would simply take it back to Laurel.

At first she couldn't find Heather at all. Heather always played four-square and dominated the game. Today Margaret only saw Katie playing with some of Heather's friends. She looked over at the benches. Sometimes Heather and her followers gathered there to whisper about people, but today the benches were empty. Clyde still had a group of kids around him, but Heather wasn't there either. Margaret got off the swing and sauntered around the playground. The day was cloudy and bleak with a slight drizzle. Even though it was miserable out, Margaret noticed that the wetness made the crystals in the blacktop shine.

Then she spotted Heather standing slumped up against the school building staring out across the empty baseball field. Margaret had never seen Heather alone before. It was rather a shock. Heather looked withered up and small. Margaret approached Heather slowly, and when Heather saw her she turned her face away and looked down at her loafers.

"I suppose," she said glumly as Margaret drew near, "you're here to tell me how much you hate me for ratting on you. Go ahead."

"No," Margaret replied coolly. "I wouldn't even talk to you if I absolutely didn't have to."

"Well?" Heather said, looking up. "What do you want then?"

Margaret unzipped her bib overall pocket and drew out one of the silver stars.

"Here," she said, handing the star to Heather, "this is to you from Laurel."

Heather's mouth dropped open. To Margaret's surprise she reached eagerly for the star.

"From Laurel?" Heather whispered. "He gave this to me?"

Margaret nodded. Heather stood for a long time gazing at the star in her hand.

"What does it mean?" she asked Margaret finally. "And what does he think of me?"

Margaret was so taken aback by Heather's response that for a moment she was at a loss for words. Heather's blue eyes were filled with such longing.

"Well," said Margaret, forming her words slowly, "this star allows you to land in Joona. Laurel says he still wants you to come with us."

"He does?" Heather asked incredulously. "He isn't cross?"

Margaret shook her head, bewildered. This was not the Heather she knew. The Heather she knew wouldn't have cared one iota whether Laurel was cross or not. Then to her utter shock Heather slipped the star over her neck.

"Then I shall go!" she exclaimed, a smile beginning to spread across her solemn face. "I shall go with you tonight! I still have another chance and no one will stop me this time. Not even myself."

The bell for the end of recess screamed out over the playground. Heather seemed not to hear. She was looking down at her silver star and fingering it fondly. Kids were running by them from all directions to get back into the building, but Heather seemed oblivious. Margaret didn't quite know what to do and almost left Heather there, but something made her stay. Finally, they were standing alone on the silent playground.

"Heather," Margaret said finally. "Heather, the bell rang. We'll be late for class."

"I know," Heather remarked casually, not moving. "I must say I've been a beast to you, Margaret. You don't have to say anything. I'm sure I'm the last person you want coming along to Joona with you tonight. But maybe, if we get to know each other all over again in a new place, you and I . . . well, we'll see."

Margaret just stood there and blinked and blinked. She thought perhaps she was in a dream. Then she wondered if maybe Heather was feverish or going slightly mad. Then again it could all be a trick. Some devilish plan Heather had worked up to deceive her. It was hard to believe this. Heather's eyes were too bright and she was smiling with an innocent kind of charm that Margaret had never seen before.

"Well," said Margaret finally, licking her lips because they were quite dry from shock, "we really should get going."

"Yes, of course," Heather said softly. "But let's walk slowly. I want you to tell me about what happened in Joona last night. I want to know about everything I missed."

11
THE DATE

Uncle John left the house about 6:45 looking extremely handsome. At least Margaret thought so. She had helped him choose what to wear and ironed his paisley tie for him because the point at the bottom curled up. She even shined his shoes and brushed some lint off his navy blue jacket.

"I am so glad you have a date, Uncle John," Margaret told him as he was about ready to leave. "Whoever she is, she's bound to be happy when she sees you. You look macho."

Uncle John seemed embarrassed and checked the cloudy mirror in the hall.

"I haven't been on a date in so long," he said to Margaret, taking his comb out and skimming it over his wavy hair. "Is it appropriate these days to bring flowers, or is that overdoing it, do you think?"

"I think flowers would really be the clincher," Margaret said after a moment's thought. "They have some roses down at May's florist. I saw them in the window."

"So roses would be good?" Uncle John asked nervously, putting his comb back into his front jacket pocket. "I'll stop on the way down. Besides, it's not good to get there early. It makes me look too eager."

84

"Get yellow ones," said Margaret. "They're the most romantic."

"Really?" said Uncle John.

"And get half a dozen. It shows you care."

"Really?" said Uncle John.

"Aren't you going to tell me who this person is?" Margaret teased him one last time.

She'd been pestering her uncle all afternoon with questions about this mystery woman, but he appeared unwilling to dispense too much information.

"I have my reasons for not telling you anything more," Uncle John said pleasantly, "until things come together, if you know what I mean. Now, are you sure you will be all right here alone tonight?"

"I'm positive," Margaret assured him.

She couldn't wait to get going to Joona. The wan, stark faces of Samson and Priscilla loomed before her. She wanted to tell Uncle John about the cruel Regalia and about Heather, but she knew he was leaving. She didn't want him to worry about her and certainly she didn't want him to forbid her to go. She waved goodbye to him at the door as he roared off in his Jeep, churning up a cloud of dirt as he pulled away. Margaret watched the dirt billow upward. Slowly the air cleared and the dust settled down again. As it did, Margaret was shocked to see Heather Fitzgerald standing in her driveway. She had her silver star on and her school books under one arm.

"Heather!" Margaret exclaimed. "What are you doing here? We don't have to leave for at least another hour and a half."

"I know," Heather said simply. "I brought homework. But I didn't want to be late and I didn't want to go there alone. Craig is mad at me and won't talk to me."

"Well," Margaret replied flustered, "why don't you just come in and wait? Ryan's coming by here about eight. We'll leave then."

"Are you sure that's early enough?" Heather asked, worried. "I mean, I don't want to miss that swan."

"You won't miss him," Margaret assured her. "Besides, Laurel would never leave without us."

Heather went in and the two of them sat on the couch for a while silently doing their homework. Neither of them spoke. It was so strange having Heather Fitzgerald sitting in her living room that Margaret could not concentrate on her story problems. Finally she nervously rose to her feet and blurted out, "Would you like some cocoa?"

Heather nodded and Margaret got up to fix some. When she came back into the living room with two mugs Heather had her face in her hands. She was sniffing and her shoulders were heaving up and down. Margaret had never seen Heather cry before. She didn't know Heather had tears. She set the mugs on the coffee table and sat across from Heather in the wicker rocking chair. She didn't know what to do or say, so she just watched while Heather cried. Eventually Heather began to calm down, found her voice, and began to talk in short, breathy sentences.

"Why on earth are you being so nice to me?" she gasped between sobs. "You have no right to treat me nicely. I didn't ever treat you nicely."

Margaret shrugged awkwardly. She had no idea why she had invited Heather in and made her cocoa. It had just sort of happened that way without her thinking about it.

"I'm not being that nice," Margaret countered. "I'm just being a little bit nice. It's very strange having you in my living room."

"I'm sorry," said Heather tearfully, beginning to gather her things. "I shouldn't have come."

"No," Margaret explained. "That's not what I mean. You and me, Heather, we were enemies. We were fighting like cats just yesterday morning. And now here you are sitting in my house."

"I wanted to go with you last night," Heather said softly. "More than anything I wanted to go to Joona with that swan. I stood there by the swinging bridge after you had taken off and I felt like I had missed something I desperately wanted. And then, when you gave me this star, I felt like things had changed. Like I got a second chance. I've never gotten a second chance before."

"A second chance," Margaret said quietly, matching Heather's tone, "to a new world you can hardly believe is possible. But it is possible. With Laurel, anything is possible."

"Shouldn't we leave?" Heather asked again nervously. "I don't want to miss him."

Margaret sighed and looked up at the clock. It was only seven fifteen.

"I suppose I could call Ryan and tell him we'll meet him there."

Even though Heather was being a bit annoying, Margaret herself was anxious to get going. She couldn't bear the thought of Samson and Priscilla suffering one moment longer than necessary. She picked up the receiver and pressed in Ryan's number. Ryan answered.

"I'll meet you there," she said softly into the phone. "We're leaving early. Heather is here."

"Gee whiz, lucky you. What's she doing there?"

"No, it's all right," Margaret assured him. "She's coming with us tonight."

"I guess we're in for it then," Ryan said. "My mother just left, so I can leave early too. I'm dying to help out those swans. Couldn't sleep a wink last night."

"Did Theodore get back?"

"No, I think he stayed over in Joona. My mother's used to

him disappearing now and then. She doesn't really worry all that much if he misses a night at home."

A thought occurred to Margaret and she almost put it out of her head. Then she said slowly, "Ryan, you don't happen to know where your mother went this evening, do you?"

"She said she had a date with some guy. Wouldn't tell me who. He came by and gave her a bunch of roses and then they left. I didn't see him. I was up in my room, but the roses are here on the table. They're yellow ones. Six of them."

Even though they were early, Laurel was waiting for them. Margaret and Heather got there first. Laurel was sitting along the bank preening himself and rose to his feet when he saw them.

"Heather!" Laurel called as soon as he saw her come into view. "I am so glad you could make it. I've been thinking about you a great deal. Our adventure wouldn't be complete without you."

"Really?" asked Heather, astounded at the swan's friendliness. "I'm sorry about last night. I didn't want to...."

"Never mind," Laurel piped. "It's like water off a duck's back. Do sit down, both of you. I am glad to see you are both wearing your stars."

They sat down cross-legged in the grass and the swan nestled himself down as well.

"I didn't know you got here early," Margaret said. "Otherwise I would have come early all the time, just to talk."

Laurel bent his neck down and looked Margaret in the eye with deep affection. Finally he lay his head in her lap. She stroked the top of his head gently. It was soft and smooth and warm.

"I don't always get here early," the swan said after a time.

"It all depends which way the currents take me. Today the wind was at my back and I filled up on Joona water. I knew I would need the extra strength to carry four. I had a hunch Heather might be coming along too. Oh, Heather, I almost forgot!"

Laurel put his bill under his wing and pulled out something that was wet, brown, and flat.

"I think," suggested the swan, "this might belong to your father? I found it downriver a ways, caught in between two rocks."

Heather's eyes grew wide.

"Oh Laurel!" she exclaimed, opening the brown flat object. "Why, this is my father's wallet! However did it get...."

Then she paused.

"Oh yes," she continued sheepishly. "I remember now. Last night he lost something out of his front pocket and didn't know what it was. Funny. He doesn't usually keep his wallet in his front shirt pocket at all."

"Which is probably why he didn't know what he'd lost," Laurel suggested kindly. "I am amazed that you landbred creatures can keep track of all the things you carry around with you—purses, sunglasses, lunch boxes, school books, even clothing. It must get cumbersome. I've had a time of it just now keeping this wallet—if that's what you call it—tucked under my wing. It makes moving about much less efficient."

The swan paused a moment and lifted his head.

"Well, yet another early bird. Here comes Ryan."

As he came across the bridge Margaret met Ryan's eyes and smirked. Ryan grinned back and then blew out a low whistle.

"You'll never believe it, Laurel," Margaret told the swan. "Uncle John is dating Wilda tonight—Ryan's mom."

"Yeah," said Ryan, joining them, "and not only that. He bought her roses!"

"That's because I told him to," Margaret confessed somewhat obligingly.

"Splendid!" Laurel declared, looking fondly at both of them. "I thought your uncle needed a bit of uplifting. They will be well suited for each other, I'm sure."

"Perhaps," Margaret said, and cleared her throat, "but what about the two of us and Theodore? If they get married it means. . . ."

"Don't count your cygnets before they hatch," Laurel interjected mildly. "It's only their first date."

"What are cygnets?" asked Margaret.

"Baby swans?" Heather ventured.

"Right you are!" Laurel affirmed. "And they are not ugly either, as one of your landbred reading classics asserts."

Ryan looked skeptically at Heather.

"Gee whiz, Heather. We certainly don't need you spreading information about this love affair all over the school, although you probably will just to make yourself look knowledgeable."

"No I won't," Heather said sincerely.

"Well," Ryan replied, a bit flustered by the simplicity of Heather's response. "We'll see about that."

"Hey! There's Craig!" Margaret announced. "We're all here."

"Thought I'd come a little bit early," Craig said and snorted. His nose had stuffed up again since returning from Joona.

"Thought I'd be the first one here, too," he continued. "Good gosh! What's she doing here?" he asked, pointing at his sister.

Heather looked down and mangled a piece of grass between her thumb and forefinger.

"She's coming along tonight," Laurel told him gently. "And she is quite welcome, although I can understand how the past could distort your view of the present. It is a pity this happens so often."

"I'm not talking to her," Craig announced, and flung himself down on the ground in a pout.

"Do keep your sense of humor, dear boy," Laurel encouraged, going over to Craig and lifting his chin up with the tip of his beak. "It's going to be quite fine, I assure you."

"Let's get on with it!" Margaret interjected. "I can't bear the thought of Samson and Priscilla being tormented for one moment longer. Please, Laurel, take us to them now and take us quickly."

"Exactly what I would propose," Laurel agreed. "There's much work to be done and the sooner we leave the greater the gain. Hop on now, everyone, and keep your spirits up, Craig. Life is lived in the now. Do accept my apologies for the tight squeeze back there with four, but I'm sure you'll manage."

It was a tight squeeze but not uncomfortable. Heather's eyes were wide. She sat next to Margaret and clung to her arm the entire trip. Ryan and Craig sat behind. To Margaret's surprise, Laurel had no problem taking off. The air was brisk and cold against her cheeks and the wind must have shifted direction, for it was pushing them on from behind.

"A lovely night," Laurel announced once they were airborne. "A perfectly delightful evening. Hardly a star that isn't twinkling with laughter. Nearly a full moon. The wind, thankfully, is at our backs again and we should make good time."

"Look, Margaret!" Heather gasped. "Look how close the stars are! Why I could almost touch them!"

"I know," Margaret said, nodding her admiration at the stars. "It's like they were made of sugar."

"And the lights below, Margaret! Clusters of them all twinkling! It's gorgeous up here and so very . . . so very quiet."

Heather cocked her head as if listening to the silence. The

only sound was the flapping of Laurel's wings and the whoosh of the wind as it blew them across the sky.

"You never liked it silent before!" Craig blurted out from behind them. "You always play that loud music and wear your earphones when there's nothing going on. You always said that the quiet made you nervous!"

"This is different," Heather said almost reverently. "This is beautiful."

"Glad you're enjoying your flight!" Laurel rejoined, sailing down an air current and climbing back up again. "It is glorious, isn't it? I can't see how you landbred creatures can bear to be grounded all the time!"

"We don't know anything better," Ryan sighed. "When you don't know anything better, it's hard to imagine something this thrilling. It's sort of like being born blind. You can never really know what color something is."

"It is a pity," Laurel agreed.

"Laurel," Margaret asked, with concern in her voice, "have any more dreadful things happened since we left Joona?"

"More of the same," Laurel called back. "A few more swans taken prisoner, and a few more of the Regalia guarding the front door of the castle. You have many great supporters in the troop of swans that are in hiding. Theodore has outlined a plan for them. They are finally cooperating and are somewhat organized. We will stop there first and fill you in to make sure we've got our signals straight."

"How is my mother?" asked Margaret. "I haven't gotten to see her yet."

"She is safe," Laurel assured her. "And eager to see you. But she mustn't come out until all is at peace. It would be too risky for her, being the queen."

Margaret nodded and fell silent. And if they failed? If they didn't bring peace? Would they join the ranks of the prisoners in the castle dungeon, destined to carry heavy loads on their backs and waste away under the cruel rule of the Regalia? Would Joona then be destroyed and the water become polluted with the green mire of jealousy? Would the boundaries be set in place to exclude those who were poor and suffering and unfit for the Regalia's purposes? And Laurel? What would become of him? What would keep the Regalia from hypnotizing all of them like they had done to Alexander? That would be the worst of all. Then she would go about doing all sorts of wicked, cruel things at their beck and call that she had no desire to do. The Regalia had already taken so many of Joona's own swans for its prisoners, slaves, and soldiers. Thinking about the enormity of the task that lay ahead of them made her head spin. The Regalia frightened her, and there was little she could do to keep herself from being nervous. She was on edge for the remainder of the flight, lost in her thoughts. The others had fallen silent also, and Margaret wondered if perhaps they too were as apprehensive as she was.

12
THE DOOR
IN THE ROCK

Margaret felt her ears pop and realized they were already descending toward the cave. She took the key out of her pocket and as soon as they landed she ran over and unlocked the door. The others followed. The rush of happy, bubbling water met them, and then Margaret noticed four canteens sitting on the bank.

"The canteens are for you," Laurel told them. "Fill them with Joona water and keep them in your possession. Drink some too. It will strengthen you and put you in high spirits."

Margaret hardly needed an invitation. She was thirsty. Her mouth had gone dry and stayed that way ever since she had given Heather her star on the playground. Now she knelt on the bank with the others and put her mouth and half her face into the rushing water. It tasted sweet and gave her light tingles as it swept through her insides. The river was rushing so fast that it splattered her forehead and drenched her hair. Ryan cupped his hands and washed his face. Then he stuck his arms down in the water and whooshed a huge wave over at Margaret. The wave jumped the bank and drenched her completely.

"Gee whiz, Margaret!" Ryan teased. "Just thought I should

practice treating you like my sister in case your uncle and my mom get married."

Margaret, feeling suddenly quite playful as well, walked over to Ryan and poured her full canteen of water over his head.

"I suppose I should practice as well!" she giggled. "Just in case."

Ryan turned and grabbed Margaret around her waist. Margaret yelped, but before she knew what was happening Ryan had dragged her into the river up to her knees. The water was wonderfully blue and inviting and in her playful, inquisitive frame of mind Margaret could not contain herself.

"Oh well," she sighed as Ryan continued to splash her, "if you can't beat 'em, join 'em."

Without a second thought, she plunged into the rushing river. The force of the swift current caught her immediately and pulled her against her will under the water. Margaret could hear the muffled roar of the river above her. Despite her futile efforts to beat the current she felt strangely peaceful as she saw bubbles fizzing up around her and seaweed swaying against her arms. Then something caught her and she seemed to be spinning around in a spiral that swirled her up, up, up until she bobbed to the surface again. Margaret coughed and sputtered. She was moving forward at an awesome pace. She saw the others quite a distance off jumping up and down on the bank and yelling things at her she couldn't make out. When she finally looked up she saw Laurel flying above her and realized, to her surprise, that she wasn't in the least bit afraid. She felt wonderful.

"Hi, Laurel!" she called, waving at the swan. "This is sensational. Something is holding me up like I'm sitting in an inner tube."

"Joona water always will hold you up," Laurel called down to her with a lilt in his voice. "The circular springs that feed

Joona's waters act as buoys. I knew you'd be up for air in a moment. Your spirits have lifted too, and I must say, you look so comfortable in the water that if I didn't know you, I might not believe you were really a landbred creature at all."

"Do I look like a swan then?" Margaret called back, delighted. She took Laurel's observation as a compliment.

"You swim as well as one," Laurel conceded. "Although your head is not feathery enough. Now Margaret, as soon as you get to the quiet pool by the waterfall, wait for us. We will be by to pick you up there. The others are not as daring as you and wish to ride the river on my back. I must be getting back to them. They will be wondering what became of you."

"I was scared of the Regalia before we got here, but I'm not anymore," Margaret said calmly, bobbing through some white caps. "They can't be that hard to handle. After all, we have you and Milohe and the rainbow on our side."

"You most certainly do, my dear," Laurel assured her. "I shall be going now. If you should stop for any reason before the quiet pool, be sure to stay in plain view so we can find you. Don't wander. We will meet you by the falls, if not before, momentarily."

Margaret nodded. Laurel swooped around and flew back. Margaret watched as he disappeared around a craggy bend in the cave. Her body was relaxed and limp in the water, but her mind was excited. She felt as though she ought to tell the leaders of the Regalia a thing or two, face to face. Maybe that would straighten them out. If it didn't, maybe she ought to slug the leader in the beak and pluck out a few of his feathers. Then he'd know how it felt. Who did he think he was, anyway, wrecking this wonderful paradise for swans? She was prepared to take them on—all of them! Joona water was the trick. It always gave her courage.

She reached down and felt her canteen up against her waist. Luckily she had clipped it there just after she poured the water on Ryan's head. Her silver star was around her neck tucked in behind her overall bib, and the key and the magic feather were safe inside her zippered pocket. Margaret was glad she had the presence of mind to always wear overalls. They were so convenient.

Presently she came to the quiet pool by the waterfall. Here she stopped bobbing around and simply floated. She thought she might like to get out and wait for the others on a rock, and after a bit of a struggle she managed to stand up. Her overalls, convenient as they might be, were heavy when they were wet, and she slogged over to the bank a bit off balance. Still, she made it up to a mossy rock and watched the tall, frothy waterfall thunder down at her. Filling up her canteen with water she sat comfortably back on the rock.

This was where they had first seen Laurel again after he had been shot by Craig's father. She remembered the fun they had chasing each other in the pool and Laurel's ecstacy at being with them again that day. Then he had taken them to Joona and there had been beautiful music filling the air and myriads of shining swans floating below them and singing glorious words up at them. She must do something to restore Joona to its proper state. It wasn't meant to be so silent and empty. It wasn't a place where whistles and commands were meant to pierce the air. She missed the music.

A voice from nowhere jolted Margaret from her thoughts. Someone was shouting commands from somewhere underneath her. The words were muffled but the tone of voice was abrasive and abrupt. The voice was quite loud, for she could hear it over the waterfall's roar. Normally she would have been rather frightened, but Joona water was pulsing through her veins and Margaret felt courageous. Looking back down the river from where she had come, she did not spot the others. Gingerly she got to her feet and began to look around. The rocks were slippery and she found it difficult to move about.

Since the voice seemed to be coming from beneath her she was at a loss as to where to begin. Still, she began to climb in search of a clue. Without realizing she had gone so far, she suddenly found herself within arm's reach of the falls.

The sound from the waterfall was deafening here and the shouting voice she had heard seemed to have vanished. A soft mist from the falls sprayed her already damp face with airy, light bubbles and the water churned somersaults around the slippery black rock where she stood. Margaret was about to turn back, for she knew the others could not spot her. She had climbed around some rather large boulders to get to where she was, and her view of the river was blocked as well. Then she heard a loud, abrasive shout against the backdrop of the thunderous falls.

There was a hole in the cave's ceiling at the top of the falls. Bright light always shone down through it in thick, golden rays. It could not be the earth's sunlight, for it was nighttime on earth just now, but its appearance was just the same. Long beams of transparent gold reached down and made the water dazzle as if it were made of diamonds. Margaret paused to notice the lovely way the light played against the water. As she did, a peculiar thing caught her eye. The light, glittering against the shimmering water, caught something else behind the falls. She would never have seen it had she not been standing at this precise angle. Margaret blinked and took a step forward. It was no mirage. Behind the falls stood a black glossy rock, and hinged to the rock was a lime-green door.

13
THE
PLAN

Ryan, Craig and Heather, astride Laurel's back, looked for Margaret for a good hour in the passageway, tracing and retracing their course. Finally, Laurel suggested they give up the search.

"I am sure she made her way safely to Joona," he offered hopefully. "We will most certainly see her there."

"Suppose the Regalia have her?" Ryan whispered. "They could have captured her, you know. It's all my fault. I shouldn't have teased her."

Heather pursed her lips and her eyes grew wide. Craig just shook his head soberly.

"Maybe she's one of them now," he muttered. "All hypnotized and spacey."

"She's got the magic feather," Ryan said. "That might keep her out of danger."

They were sitting astride Laurel's back in an alcove not far from the entrance to Joona. The current was not swift in this side pool. This was the third time they had stopped here in their search for Margaret. Above them was a little ceiling that dripped water on their heads.

"Swans are curious creatures," Laurel said pensively after

a moment's pause. "They get hunches or impressions of things. It's the only way they know where to dunk their head for seaweed, or which way to turn in the heavens to reach a certain destination here on earth. As to Margaret, I have such a hunch, and it's a strong one. I think she will be better assisted if we move on now according to plan. If we haven't found her here yet, we probably won't, and we mustn't waste time. If she has been taken by the Regalia she will need our help immediately. On the other wing, she may be safely to Joona already, ahead of us."

"Move on then," Ryan consented with a nod.

"We've already looked everywhere, anyway," Craig agreed. "There's not much more we can do now."

Laurel began to flap his wings and in moments they were airborne. They flew for a short time through the cave and then broke out into the rainbow light of Joona. Heather gasped.

"A rainbow!" she cried as they entered the purple band and streaked through it to the crimson. "A virtual masterpiece of color! It's like liquid, all moving and shining."

They flew through the crimson band for a while and then Laurel shot out of the rainbow into the open sky.

"Stay low," he called back to the children. "This is the dangerous section. We have no cover. We must cross over to that little island."

They were moving quickly. Ryan couldn't remember a time when Laurel had flown faster. The swan's wings were beating the air with a rapid "pom, pom, pom," and the cool Joona breezes whipped at his face. Keeping his head down, Ryan managed to peer over the swan's right shoulder and catch a glimpse of the island. It was a small clump of deep green in the middle of the sea with only two pine trees on it. Nothing impressive about it except that beyond it loomed the great stone castle piercing upward with its tall pointy towers and slate roofs. Last time when he had been to Joona the place had appeared friendly and inviting, like a well-constructed castle in a child's sandbox. Now it looked foreboding and frightening as if it had been painted a dark color and all its smooth edges filed into sharp ones.

"We're very near to the castle," Laurel called to them softly, and Ryan barely heard him. "Keep low and don't say a word. The place is swarming with the Regalia. When we land, stay close."

They approached the island now and flew just above the water.

"Over there!" Craig whispered hoarsely into Laurel's ear. "A Regalia swan!"

They all looked out. Next to a lilac bush fairly close to the shore stood a large swan with an orange beak. He had definitely seen them and was waving at them with his wing like he was directing traffic.

"He probably wants to trick us," Craig whispered again. "Making us think he's friendly."

"Good spot," Laurel called back to him softly. "But there's no need to be concerned. It's Alexander come to meet us. Probably a bit ruffled because we're late."

They swooped down and Laurel made a virtually noise-less landing along the bank, drawing up a few feet from Alexander. The children jumped off and Alexander put his wing to his beak. It didn't look quite the same as when some-one puts a finger to his lips, but they all knew what it meant— "Be quiet." He paused a moment.

"Where's Margaret?" he whispered, with a furrow in his brow.

"We lost her," Craig whispered back.

"Took a swim and disappeared in the tunnel," Laurel explained in a low voice. "I'm confident we'll retrieve her, Alexander."

"I hope so," Alexander said, his voice barely audible. "Follow me!"

As fast as a swan could waddle, Alexander led them along the grassy bank to a place where a wide gravel path began. The path curved upward to the right, and Alexander turned and went a few feet forward. Suddenly he disappeared.

"Gee whiz!" Ryan rasped.

"He's gone!" Heather mouthed.

Laurel looked back at them and motioned for them to come forward. As they did they saw that the gravel path led them between two tiny hills. In the left hill there was a small hole close to the ground partially covered by some sticks and pine cones.

"In there!" Laurel whispered. "Hurry!"

The hole hardly looked big enough for any of them. Ryan went first, intending to squeeze himself through, but once he stooped down he realized it would be unnecessary. The hole was actually much larger than it appeared from the outside. The sticks and pine cones camouflaged a whole section of the entryway and Ryan let himself in easily. Heather, Craig, and finally Laurel followed.

Blinking in the dim light Ryan noticed Alexander almost at once. Then he saw a whole group of other swans clustered together along the far wall of a large room busily discussing something. The light in the room came from four candles that hung from iron holders fastened to the wall with nails. As soon as the swans saw the children enter a hush fell over the company.

"It's the landbred creatures," Ryan heard one of them whisper. "The ones Laurel said would come to help us."

"It's two of the ones that led us to Joona through the tunnel!" another one spoke softly.

A general murmur of agreement rose up and a few swans put one wing up to their foreheads in salute.

"Margaret is missing," Laurel told them all solemnly. "We must keep a keen lookout for her."

The swans began to mutter among themselves with distressed looks on their faces.

"We will find her," Laurel assured them. "But with everyone's help we will find her much sooner."

"Ryan!" a voice boomed out that Ryan didn't recognize. "You made it!"

Ryan whirled around. There, stooped over because of the low ceiling, stood Theodore, grinning at him from ear to ear. Ryan's mouth dropped open and he ran his hand through his hair. It was the first time he had ever heard his brother's voice, if indeed it had been his brother that had spoken to him just now.

"Theo . . . Theodore," Ryan stammered. "Did you . . . just say something?"

Theodore, looking quite pleased with himself, took a step forward and put his big meaty arm around Ryan's shoulders. Craig and Heather were watching Theodore with awe.

"Did I surprise you?" Theodore asked hopefully.

His words were rich and warm. Ryan's eyes filled with tears and he wrapped his arms around his brother, burying his face in Theodore's flannel shirt. Theodore was speaking! Ryan had never realized how much he had longed to hear his brother's voice.

"What happened to you?" Ryan managed, choking back a sob.

Theodore patted Ryan on the back several times. They were hefty pats made with the flat of his thick hand.

"Nothing out of the ordinary," Theodore explained calmly. "I can always talk when I'm in Joona. A few doses of the water and I'm quite good at carrying on a conversation."

"Gee whiz, I should have figured it out!" Ryan said,

sniffing and wiping his eyes on his arm. He looked up at his brother's beaming face and grinned.

"I should have known," Ryan continued, "that if swans could talk in Joona then of course you, Theodore, could also talk here. I don't know why I didn't think of it before."

"Words mean a great deal here," Laurel said quietly, bending down low in a swan smile. "On earth it seems that at times they are used in the most disastrous ways. Too many of them cluttering up the air with noise. Here words are regarded more as great treasures to be dispensed with care. Everyone who enters Joona is given their words as a gift. To be without words is unknown here, because to be without words is to be without expression, and to be without expression is to be less than alive."

"In fact, if I may," interrupted Alexander cautiously, "has not Milohe named you, Laurel, Ruler of Joona, his word?"

Laurel flashed a look of surprise at Alexander.

"You have spoken a secret Alexander," Laurel said in hushed tones. "It is quite all right of course, this time. The present company hears with understanding, I am sure. To your question, Alexander, yes, I am the expression of Milohe himself."

As he said this silence fell over the room and Laurel, standing under one of the candles on the wall, seemed to glow.

"Which is why," Ryan ventured finally, breaking the stillness, "we mustn't let the Regalia go on like this. They're enslaving the swans by brainwashing them. No one can express themselves if they're brainwashed!"

"In a way," Heather said softly, for she was very timid now in her new surroundings, "it's almost as if the Regalia have a kind of blindness. They don't know who they are."

"Precisely, dear," Laurel conceded happily. "Very perceptive, Heather, and very true."

Heather looked gratefully at Laurel.

"I certainly consider myself to have been blinded during my captivity," Alexander declared, shaking his head. "Perhaps I was functioning, but I was not seeing things accurately, that's for sure."

"We should shoot them," Craig said adamantly. "Shoot every last one of them and let them rot."

"Perhaps," Alexander said slowly, "although killing something is not usually the way that Laurel works."

"Our battle plan that we've been discussing," Theodore offered in his rich deep voice, "is actually the opposite. Our battle plan is not to kill, but rather to detain and then restore. It depends on you three. Did you bring weapons with you?"

"We don't have any weapons!" Craig exclaimed. "Besides, what you say sounds pretty impossible. Killing them is a much safer way to go about this in my opinion. Maybe we could drop rocks on their heads."

"Actually," Laurel piped in, "the impossible as you see it is really quite possible."

"Yes," agreed Theodore, "and we've seen the impossible work time and time again."

The rest of the swans had been gathering around them as they were talking and they now stood in a tight circle listening to every word. Some of them had their heads cocked, others were nodding, but everyone seemed to be in general agreement about one thing: Detaining the enemy and restoring the enemy was a realistic battle plan for them, and certainly nothing to scoff at.

"This is how we thought it might work," Theodore continued. "We've been up for many hours discussing this, and I think we are on to something. We certainly don't have a moment to lose, so here it is in a nutshell. I give myself up to the Regalia. That will distract them for a time. I doubt if they have ever seen a landbred creature as large as myself. To capture me will be a great victory for them. The rest of you must infiltrate the castle. How that is done is the one drawback. It appears that every door is guarded."

"The sacred text!" Ryan exclaimed suddenly. "The scroll told us that there was a latch door for this very purpose in the left tower of the castle, hidden in the rock. It is halfway up and it is always kept unlocked. The scroll said that it hadn't been discovered yet by the enemy, so it's a sure way in."

The swans looked at Ryan with wide-eyed amazement.

"You children read the sacred text?" one of the swans asked with reverent awe. "Only a very few can read its message. You must be magicians of the highest nature."

"It wasn't us at all," Craig said, shaking his head. "It was this crimson light. But anyway, I still say this plan isn't safe. We ought to think massacre."

"This is exactly the information we needed!" Theodore said with a relieved sigh. "Lead swans! Did you hear that? Left tower, halfway up a latch door, unlocked. Did the sacred text tell you anything else? It is very important that we follow its instructions exactly."

"It said that we all have to resist together with strength!" Craig offered with a military tone to his voice.

"And something about how the enemy works," Ryan added thoughtfully. "Oh yeah, it also said that the stars of Joona were our weapons and to use them confidently. I'm not sure what that means. It never gets dark here so I have never seen the stars."

Theodore thought a moment and then began to nod his head thoughtfully.

"Perhaps I can help with that one," he offered after a few moments had elapsed. "The stars around your necks . . . Laurel gave those to the three of you for right of passage, am I correct? Hold them up."

The swans drew closer together as Ryan, Craig, and Heather held up their stars to the candlelight. Theodore examined the stars carefully, turning them round and round, rubbing them between his thumb and forefinger and tilting them up to the light. Then, taking some water from his canteen, he rubbed it on the surface of Heather's star.

"It's Joona water," he told them. "Now look, Heather. The surface of the star is a mirror. You can see yourself in it."

Heather looked into her silver star and saw her own face looking back.

"What good does that do us?" Craig groaned. "Anyone who owns a powder puff has her own mirror."

"Wait a second," Theodore said patiently. "Let me finish. Now hold your star in your right hand, Heather, and tilt it backwards at a slant so that it catches the light, just so. That's it. Aim the longest arm of the star down at the floor. Be careful not to aim it at anyone. Okay, good. Now squeeze the star ever so slightly."

As Heather applied pressure to her star, a shaft of white light shot out from the pointed tip that she had aimed at the floor. Ryan thought it looked like a comet, or better yet a laser. The steady stream of light hit the floor a few feet away from them and seemed to silently explode. The entire room flashed full of white light as if engulfed by lightning. Then it was gone.

"Goodness!" Heather gulped after a few moments of blinking to get herself adjusted to the dimness of the room again. "I had no idea I was carrying around that much power."

"Your stars were given to you by Milohe to be used as weapons as well as for right of passage," Theodore told them soberly. "Laurel's servants usually have weapons on them, although like yourselves, they may be unaware of it. I had one once, ages ago, to combat a similar situation. I'm glad my memory serves me well as to how to operate them. Please be advised these are not toys and they must be kept moist with the Joona water to work. Be very careful how you aim. The swan you aim at will become blinded by the light immediately.

107

So be absolutely certain you are aiming at an enemy, not a friend."

"Most of the Regalia wear whistles around their necks," Alexander reminded them. "If they are prisoners, they have their identification number branded into their backs."

"After we blind them, then what do we do?" Heather asked.

"We leave the restoration part up to Laurel," Theodore told her. "He will finish the task."

They all looked around to see Laurel, but the space under the candle where he had been standing was empty.

"Where did he go?" Craig asked. "We can't possibly succeed without his magic."

"His magic is with us," Alexander said, putting his wing up around Craig's shoulders to reassure him. "He had a call from someone in need. He comes and goes quite frequently. You might as well get used to it."

"He will appear again at the right time," Theodore said, completely unalarmed. "As for us, we must get going. There's not a moment to lose. Lead swans! The first three of you must each take one of the three landbred creatures on your back. Once you get inside the castle walls, split up. The rest of you shall assign yourselves to a lead swan and follow close behind. As soon as one of the Regalia has been hit, you must take over their post."

"Heather, you shall ride on me," Alexander said, waddling up to her. "I am number three in the lead and quite strong."

"Good," Heather sighed. "At least I know you a little."

"I'm leaving now," Theodore told them, putting his hand on Ryan's shoulder in a parting farewell. "Wait until you hear a whistle blowing. That means they've captured me. Then take off and fly as fast as you can toward the castle. I'm sure they'll be too preoccupied with hauling me in before Sebastian to notice much of anything else."

"Sebastian?" Ryan sputtered. "The Dark Swan? Is that the leader?"

"Disguises himself, to be sure," Theodore told him. "But it's every bit him, all right. Calls himself the Great One just now and perpetually sits in the throne room doling out punishments on whomever he pleases. Makes him feel powerful to see others wretched."

"You be careful," Ryan said, grabbing Theodore's arm.

"Yes, do!" echoed the company of swans.

"We'll be by to rescue you," promised Craig. "Sooner than you can wink an eye."

"Or shake a tail feather," blurted out Alexander.

"Thanks," Theodore said and pursed his lips. "I'm off."

He took one last look at all of them and left.

They heard the shrill, piercing shriek of a whistle about five minutes later. Sitting astride his lead swan Ryan nodded to Craig, then to Heather. They nodded back. Then, one by one, the silent army left the safety of their underground hideaway for the open sky.

14
THE ATTACK

Their silent flight was short and swift. As they approached the castle, Ryan, who was in the lead, discovered the door immediately just as the sacred writings had described it. If he hadn't known it was there he never would have noticed it. The door was made out of the same gray rock as the castle tower. Only a wiry outline of the arched door in the tower that could just as easily have been mistaken for a wandering crack gave its presence away. The door was small, about as high as an average-sized swan when standing erect.

Although he saw the door as soon as they approached the tower, Ryan wasn't quite sure what to do next. There was no place to land on the smooth surface of the tower, and the door did not appear to have a knob or a latch to pull it open. Ryan circled around the tower once but didn't want to do it again in case the Regalia should spot them. The other swans were close behind him and followed. Ryan spoke softly to his lead swan whose name, he had learned, was Evelyn. Bending down low so he could whisper in the bird's ear he rasped, "Do you see the door?"

"Of course," said Evelyn.

"Do you think you could bash it down?"

110

Evelyn twisted her neck around and looked at Ryan with alarm.

"It's not supposed to be locked," Ryan continued softly. "If you could just get up some momentum and put your feet out a little in front of you we might be able to shove it open."

"What if the door opens out instead of in?" queried Evelyn, as she began to flap her wings furiously to increase her speed.

"Then we're all in for a bit of a bang-up," Ryan said meekly.

Evelyn swung round the tower and with wide, sweeping flaps of her long wings sailed toward the door. Seconds before they reached it, Evelyn reared back and put her feet out in front of her. Ryan almost lost his balance and grabbed the base of Evelyn's neck just in time. Then he jolted forward as Evelyn's feet made contact with the stone tower. An instant later they jolted forward again as the door gave way and they sailed into the castle's dark interior.

Ryan wanted to shout but he controlled himself. He couldn't see where he was for a moment. Then he noticed the dim flickering of lamps along the walls of a curving staircase and he told Evelyn to land on one of the steps. The others flew in behind him sounding like flags fluttering in the wind, and once they got their bearings they came to rest on the steps below him.

"Good work, Ryan," Craig said too loudly. "I wasn't sure how we were going to manage that door!"

"Shhhh! We haven't a second to lose," Ryan whispered forcibly enough so the others could hear. "Those of you closer to the bottom of the stairs, go with Heather and Craig and take the lower levels. The rest of you, follow me! This is a large castle, so be sure you cover the bases carefully. And if anyone hears anything about Margaret's whereabouts, go to her directly! She could be in grave danger at this point. When we are done, let's meet in the Penance Room."

"Located in the castle dungeon," Alexander offered helpfully.

"Let's go!" Ryan ordered, running his fingers through his pointy hair one last time in preparation for battle.

They took off again, Ryan circling upward skimming the stairs, with about thirty swans in flight behind him. Heather and Craig went the other way, plummeting downward with nearly the same number of swans behind them. Ryan's ascent was steep. When they finally reached the top of the stairs Evelyn was breathing heavily. They stopped for a moment, mostly for Evelyn's sake. Before them stretched a long, red-carpeted corridor with heavy wooden doors on either side spaced evenly apart. Before they could decide what to do next, a voice that sounded like a bristle brush scrubbing on cement demanded, "Who goes there?"

Two swans with silver whistles jumped in front of them from the shadows. Their eyes were glazed but also piercing. One of the swans had a spear sticking out from under his left wing.

"We are with Laurel!" Ryan declared loudly, amazed at his own courage. "And we come in the name of Milohe to bring Joona back to its rightful state. We give you one last chance to surrender peacefully and change your loyalties. Otherwise, we will attack!"

The two guard swans put their whistles to their beaks and blew. Immediately the doors on either side of the corridor flew open and crowds of swans with whistles around their necks entered the corridor.

Ryan grabbed his star and fired. The beam of light hit the swan, holding the spear, in the face and made a kind of sizzling noise. The swan gave a hideous scream.

"I can't see!" it croaked. "Somebody, someone, I can't see!"

Ryan aimed at the other swan. The beam of light flashed brilliantly and the second swan fell back in a heap on the floor.

"Take to the air!" Ryan called to his small army behind him.

Evelyn was airborne in a moment. The swans who had emerged from the wooden doors on either side of the corridor crowded toward them like an angry wave. Ryan began to fire downward from the air at each swan going back and forth through the corridor. Then he realized that if he kept his finger depressed and did not let up, the star would continue to emit its blinding beams in rapid succession. It made the whole process much simpler. The screams from the swans below were terrifying, and the whole crowd of them began to scatter in all directions.

"They can't fly at us to defend themselves or even to retreat," Evelyn called back to Ryan in the midst of his firing. "Their wings have been clipped!"

"We need four sentries to guard this corridor," Ryan shouted to the swans behind him. "Two at the stairs, and two at the other end of the corridor."

The four swans flying directly behind Ryan took off to their new posts.

"Now we search the rooms!" Ryan yelled.

Ryan was amazed at himself but didn't have time to really think about it too much. He'd never been much of a commander and chief yet he suddenly felt very confident and wasn't second-guessing himself like he usually did. It was as if the words he said and the decisions he made were given to him a split second before he needed them.

They began to search the rooms. It was a long process. The rooms were enormous, bright, and cheerful, each painted to match one of the colors of the rainbow. In one of the rooms the Regalia had begun to paint over the bright gold walls, making them a dismal lime-green. Inside each room were rows of poorly made nests where the Regalia army slept. There were large gold-framed paintings of Joona on the wall, some depicting the sparkling water under the rainbow, some showing the swans peacefully floating or feeding. Many of them had been slashed or pecked to mutilation.

"Those are Cornelius's pictures," Evelyn informed him. "He's our resident artist. Whenever he puts a brush to his beak the most beautiful scenes emerge on canvas. I guess he'll have to paint a few more to replace the paintings that are damaged."

They found the Regalia army hiding in every imaginable place. Some were huddled in their nests, others were hidden in closets or in small adjoining rooms. In a way Ryan hated to zap them with his star. He knew they were simply under Sebastian's influence. What kept him going was the promise of Laurel's restoration.

The castle proved to be a myriad of corridors attached to one another with Regalia sentries posted at each end. Each corridor attached a series of rooms, and most of the rooms seemed to be the living quarters for the army, as they were usually filled with an array of nests. There were other rooms as well. One room at the end of an extremely long corridor looked almost like a church. It had a whole wall made of stained glass in which an enormous white swan was soaring through the sky over a tiny ball that looked like earth. In the center of the room was a large open fountain with water shooting up in the center and splashing down on three white marble tiers. The floor was made of inlaid tiles, arranged to show the pattern of purple lilacs.

"The fountain is full of Joona water," Evelyn told Ryan. "This is the room where we gather each week to celebrate things as they were meant to be."

"It's like this room is sacred," Ryan breathed lowly. "Or just very full of beauty."

Ryan took a long drink, as did the swans, and felt wonderfully refreshed. His small army had diminished to about ten, for they had moved through the corridors and replaced the Regalia sentries with Laurel's sentries at least four or five times by now. As they turned to leave, Ryan noticed something engraved in the stone by the exit.

Uprisings of power will shake this kingdom
Our lives will be put to the test
For those alone without a friend
There will be no rest.
Yet in the midst of dark despair
Where life is nearly death
Laurel who plummets the Sulphur Sea
Will awaken in us a victory.

Heather and Craig on the lower levels were having a much different experience. Their first confrontation had been at the bottom of the staircase where two large white swans were posted by an iron door that had a small window at the top. The two swans hissed venomously as soon as they saw Heather and Craig descending on them with the other swans behind. One swan blew his silver whistle immediately. The other one cried out with a warlike scream, "Beware, traitors! You have entered the territory of the Leadership!"

Then both swans took to the air and flew at Craig and Heather. Alexander ducked a vicious peck from one of them as Heather took hold of her star and shot. The beam of light exploded in the face of the Regalia swan and with a horrific howl he fell backward against the wall. The area down by the steps was not very large and all of them were poised in mid-air, flying in place. Craig shot his star at the other swan who crumpled in the air and landed in a heap on the floor.

Just then the iron door made a grating sound as someone unlocked it from inside. As the door banged open, gleaming white swans of the Leadership emerged and took to the air like jets. There seemed to be hundreds of them. Heather and

Craig began to fire their stars fast and furiously. The Leadership swans were merciless in their pecking and, being able to fly, were able to attack from any angle. Laurel's swans were no match for them, being much smaller.

"We've got to land!" Heather screamed to Craig. "There are too many of them and they're closing in!"

The children landed at the base of the staircase where they could see the battle clearly and aim their stars carefully. Most of the Leadership were carefully avoiding Craig and Heather, realizing they were the ones who held the weapons. Each time a beam of light exploded from the children's star into the faces of the Leadership the victims would give a terrible cry and fall backwards. Some of them tried to deter Heather and Craig by flying at them, but one shot from the stars would send them wobbling wildly through the air in a blinded frenzy. Many of them landed with a crash against the wall or twirled downwards in a wild spiral to the floor.

It was awkward on the stairs, and many times Craig and Heather had to pause before shooting their stars for fear they might hit one of their own swans. The cries of Laurel's swans from the pecks of the Regalia mingled with the screams of the blinded as they echoed through the stone tower. It made the place sound like an asylum. Heather noticed blood dripping down on the step in front of her and looked up to see one of their own swans, a few steps up, bleeding profusely from the side.

Finally, after what seemed like an eternity, the last of the Regalia swans were taken down. Looking over their sorry little troop, Heather sighed.

"Some of our swans are badly wounded," she said softly.

Craig was already kneeling by the swan with the bleeding side.

"Get out your canteen and give them some of your Joona water, quickly," he told her. "It will help."

They poured the liquid down the throats of some and poured it over the heads of others. It didn't take long before the swans began to perk up. The swan with the bleeding side was the first to suggest they move on. His bleeding had stopped with a good dose of Joona water and his eyes were bright.

"I say we move on," he cackled, "before another army of those hideous Leadership find us."

"Okay!" said Heather. "Let's go."

They took off again and made their way through the iron door into a great empty room that looked like the residence of the Regalia. Here the nests that lined the wall were made of golden straw and each nest was equipped with its own satin pillow and brocade coverlet. On the wall was a portrait. When Craig saw it he gasped.

"Heather," he managed hoarsely as they flew through the room. "That's Sebastian. See how he's got that greenish tint to his feathers?"

Heather nodded. Across the bottom of the portrait were stenciled words in bold black: "The Great One."

"It looks as though he's almost like a kind of a god or something," she remarked as they flew through the empty room and out another door into still another corridor.

"He's a jerk!" Craig spat out. "He does dark magic."

"Look," Alexander said. "The door to the right. It says 'Penance Room' on it."

"Good for you, Alexander!" Craig declared. "You not only talk well, you read well too! Let's go, everyone. To the Penance Room! Quickly! It's time to rescue Samson and Priscilla and all the other prisoners from their torment."

Alexander landed and Heather disembarked to open the door. It swung open easily enough when she pulled it toward her and revealed a narrow, stone staircase that curved downward. Craig and the other swans swooped through ahead of her, and Heather, once again mounted on Alexander, brought up the rear. She heard Craig holler below her, "In the name of Laurel and by the will of Milohe!"

Before she reached the Penance Room she smelled the stink of sulfur. Then the heaviness of the heat hit her like a bomb. She could hear the laser from Craig's star already being shot. It made a light, fizzing noise and a distant sort of hum. Flying into the Penance Room, clouded with sulfuric smoke, she heard a voice calling. At first she thought it was a cry from one of the blinded swans. Then she realized someone was addressing them.

"It's Priscilla," Alexander said, looking down. "I'd know that voice anywhere."

Alexander landed again, and a very dilapidated swan came running up to them.

"Priscilla!" Alexander exclaimed. "I am so glad you are still alive."

He nuzzled Priscilla with his beak.

"Thank goodness you've come," Priscilla responded gratefully. "They were just lining us up to feed us to the lake of sulfur one by one. But I haven't time to chat."

She looked up at Heather warily.

"She is one of us?" Priscilla asked Alexander. "I don't recognize her."

"Very much so," Alexander assured her.

"Well then, you must be off at once. They have taken Margaret to the Great One and I don't know what will become of her. You must hurry."

"To his quarters?" Alexander asked.

"I'm assuming so," Priscilla wagered. "They left about ten minutes ago and I've been worried sick. There's no telling what sort of torture they might put her through."

"C'mon, Alexander!" Heather pleaded. "Hurry! Take me to Margaret this instant!"

118

15

THE PENANCE ROOM

Once Margaret had seen the green door behind the waterfall she was determined to find out what was behind it. She had gone toward it almost immediately, walking on a narrow, slippery ledge of rock. She could see that if she edged along sideways it would bring her right to the door without drenching her. It angled behind the falls in such a way that she only had to go under a very meager spray and not directly through the thick of the falling water. The ledge was difficult to maneuver and hardly wide enough at times for her to keep her balance.

She was only going to peek inside, she told herself, and she meant it. Never did she intend on staying for more than a second, for she knew that by now the others must be looking for her.

Eventually, after what seemed like ages to Margaret, she reached the small, lime-green door. It was standing partway open, and in front of it was an outcropping rock. From a distance the rock had looked pointed and jagged, but as she neared it Margaret gratefully discovered that part of it was level and broad. She hopped over to it and felt her whole body

119

relax. Thankfully, it was easy to stand on this rock and she did not have to worry about keeping her balance.

Tentatively she approached the green door and peered around the jamb. She couldn't see anything except murky, still darkness. It looked as though the door led to the middle of nowhere. Margaret opened the door a little wider to let more light in, but it didn't seem to help. She turned away in disappointment. She hoped she might have discovered something important. Then she stopped short. There was the voice again, loud and commanding. It was definitely coming from somewhere behind the door. Even the falls couldn't drown it out. She turned around and opening the door a little wider cautiously took a few steps inside.

Margaret was sure she had never been in a place quite as black and silent as this before. She couldn't see at all, even though the door behind her stood open to the light. Then she became aware of a pungent odor. The closest thing she could think of to describe it later was what it might smell like if you mixed stale potatoes with burning shoe leather. Margaret felt her stomach turn and she was convinced she didn't want to explore this putrid hole any longer. She turned to go, but as she did, two things happened.

The first was that the voice yelled out again. It was very loud and seemed to echo from way below. Someone was bellowing, but what the person said she couldn't make out. The echo was too jarring and the words were muffled. The second thing that happened was that Margaret lost her footing. She had been standing on the edge of something and as she turned to go she slipped off it. She clawed at the yawning darkness, trying to find something to hang onto. It was no use. She was falling down and falling fast. Yet she was not falling against things. Rather she was hurtling through what appeared to be completely empty space. The horrible smell grew stronger and her head began to pound from the pressure. Then with a painful jolt she landed face down on something that felt like sand.

Margaret sputtered. She had a mouth full of grit, and even though her Joona water was helping her to be brave, she was still a little bit frightened.

The odor was stronger here and the air was stifling. Margaret was a bit winded from landing so heavily on her stomach and found it difficult to breathe for a few minutes. Then she heard the voice again, or rather the voices. Strong, angry voices yelling things she still couldn't make out. Looking up she saw an opening only about thirty feet away from her and there was light on the other side. Like before, the light didn't help her to see any better, but it was a great relief to know she wasn't trapped at the bottom of some pit.

Gradually she sat up, nursing a sore elbow. A sudden thought grabbed her attention and she knew with terrifying, gut-wrenching certainty that she was in Sebastian's domain. Hadn't Laurel warned her that the star would give her right of passage anywhere? Hadn't he said on their first journey that Sebastian inhabited the dark portions of the caves that were neither part of earth nor Joona? Wasn't that lime-green door Sebastian's color—the same color as the writing on the cave wall on their first journey here? She had fallen down one of his horrid tunnels and where she was now she had no idea. Why hadn't she thought of it before? It was her own fault for being so bold and brazen and getting separated from Laurel and the others. She should have stayed put and waited before striking out on her own. Laurel could have explained the loud voice to her and saved her this misery.

Slowly she began to crawl toward the light. Whatever was at the end of it was better than this dark eerie place. She hadn't the least idea how she was going to get out of this predicament, and she hoped with all her might that the light was an exit back to the falls. She missed the others terribly.

Oddly enough, she even missed Heather. There was something coming out of Heather that was likable that hadn't been there before. Something simple and innocent. She wished Heather were with her. She wished anyone were with her. This was the first time she could ever remember having been lost, and she didn't like the feel of it one bit.

As she neared the light her body froze in mid-motion. She could hear sharp, commanding voices screaming orders and blowing whistles. So that was what she had heard by the falls! She was surrounded by the Regalia. Her heart started to pound in her throat. "Company, halt!" she heard someone yell. There was a shrill whistle and another command she couldn't make out.

Lying low to the ground, she inched her way along and peered out the opening. She was at ground level, and looking straight out she saw a long line of swans marching toward her with heavy loads on their backs. The walls behind them were made of large gray rocks and there were tiny windows far up at the top. Margaret recognized the place immediately. It was the Penance Room, the same room they had seen through the window in the crimson band of the rainbow. She remembered that Alexander had told her this was where the disobedient and rejected swans were kept, destined to live lives doing hard labor and endure all manner of abuse from the others. This meant she had somehow gotten herself inside the castle through an unguarded entrance.

The swans were close to her, barely three feet away, marching limply along. All of them had black numbers branded into their backs. Their eyes were on the ground and some of them had their feathers partially plucked out revealing bright pink skin. Others had cuts around their eyes where they had been ruthlessly pecked, and one of the swans was dragging its left wing.

"Priscilla!"

Margaret called out the swan's name before even thinking. Priscilla lifted her drooping head slightly and saw Margaret. Her eyes flashed recognition. Before Margaret knew what was happening, Priscilla had bolted from the line. In a frenzy she crawled into the hole where Margaret was hiding and lay in a heap, panting desperately.

"They'll miss me," she declared in a panic. "I know they'll miss me, but I don't care. You must get out of here or . . . or they'll kill you."

"I've come by accident," Margaret told her softly, stroking the poor bird's scrawny head. "But Laurel and the others are planning an attack and then you shall go free."

"Well, they'd better hurry," Priscilla said, glancing nervously out the opening. "Word has it that all prisoners are to be thrown into the lake of sulfur today. The Penance Room is getting too crowded. See the lake, Margaret? Out that way, it's the big steaming thing in the middle."

Margaret saw it. How could she miss it? Great clouds of sulfuric smoke rose to the ceiling and filled the room with a cloudy mist.

"This place absolutely reeks of it," Priscilla went on in an anxious whisper. "I'm only here because I couldn't be hypnotized. They don't like those sort of swans. Oh, to have Joona back the way it was meant to be! How I miss the shining rainbow and the clear cool water against my feathers and webbed feet."

"You shall be free, indeed!" Margaret assured Priscilla. "Where is Samson?"

"He was ill this morning and couldn't move," Priscilla said somberly. "They've put him in the discard pile to die. He needs water, and they won't give him any."

"I have water," Margaret told Priscilla eagerly. "It's Joona water."

Priscilla's dull eyes lit up with hope. Margaret fished around for her canteen.

"Here," she said, unscrewing the top. "Take some for yourself first."

Priscilla took a long drought.

"I could drink it forever," she said dreamily.

Margaret let some water pour over Priscilla's head and then rubbed some on her broken wing. The swan seemed to revive a bit.

"Now," instructed Margaret, "take some to Samson in your mouth. As much as you can carry."

"Number 82 is missing!" a stilted voice cried out suddenly. Then a shrill whistle pierced the air.

"That's me!" gasped Priscilla. "They've noticed I'm gone! They're sure to torture me!"

"I'll see to them," Margaret told Priscilla firmly. "Drink this and go!"

She put the canteen to Priscilla's lips and the swan emptied almost half of what was there and held it in until her cheeks bulged out. Priscilla looked at Margaret with panic in her eyes, unsure of what to do next.

"I'll distract them," Margaret told her quickly. "Your job is to get to Samson as soon as you can."

With sudden resolve leaping into her eyes, Priscilla charged back through the opening in time to catch the end of the line of swans as it was marching past. She looked up gratefully at Margaret, and for a moment all seemed to be fine.

"There's Number 82!" cried a skinny, scruffy, sharp-eyed swan with a red whistle around his neck. "Out of place! That's twenty pecks in the face!" The scruffy, sharp-eyed swan moved in on Priscilla. Margaret hopped out of the opening and gave a loud hoot.

"Excuse me, sir," she yelled at him a bit nervously. "Is this the way to Joona?"

124

The scruffy, sharp-eyed swan turned abruptly and nearly fell backwards when he saw Margaret.

"You fool!" he spat out.

Margaret gasped. She recognized the swan almost at once, although he certainly didn't look himself. It was Hector, the one they had rescued from the Regalia before. She was horrified. All the warmth was gone from his eyes. Instead they were cold and piercing like steel daggers. He proceeded to look Margaret over as if she had two heads.

"It's me, Hector!" Margaret attempted, although she had a sinking feeling it was no use. "Margaret! Remember? Theodore and I helped you to come to Joona, Hector."

"Another landbred creature in our camp," Hector muttered with a remote, monotone voice. There was not even a flicker of recognition in his stony face. "There's just been one reported to have come in upstairs. A large one!"

Margaret noticed that same pasty glaze over Hector's eyes that had been over Alexander's. Hector was waddling rapidly toward her.

"Are you alone, or did others come with you, creature?" he sneered at her.

"I'm by myself, Hector," Margaret said softly.

"Stop calling me that! You shall call me Number 52. How did you get in here?" demanded Hector with hostile bewilderment, glancing about. He was standing directly in front of her now and staring her down. Margaret looked away and saw Priscilla scuttle off out of sight, the water still making bulging pockets in her cheeks. She sighed. Now Samson would at least have a chance for survival until they were all rescued.

"Answer me!" Hector commanded, shoving his scruffy head in Margaret's face. "Or you shall be punished!"

"I fell in," Margaret told him honestly, "and came through there."

She turned around and pointed behind her to a dark

jagged hole in the castle wall. Hector was joined by other members of the Regalia who came to stare at Margaret. The swans were all rather thin and scrawny and had whistles hanging around their necks.

"You came through the Great One's tunnel?" Hector shouted at her. "Impossible! No one who enters the Great One's fortress ever comes out alive. Besides, the door is always locked. You are lying!"

The other swans drew closer to Margaret until their beaks were nearly in her face. Several of them hissed at her. Then she felt some painful pecks on the back of her neck. One of the swans had begun to attack her and was aiming for more. Margaret whirled around and faced him.

"Get your nasty beak off me!" she demanded.

She put her hand to her neck and it felt sticky and wet. When she looked down at her hand she saw there was blood on it.

"Hold your fire, Number 33!" Hector commanded, with a searing look at Margaret. "Let the Great One handle this fool creature's punishment. He will deal with her in a far more severe manner. We don't want to ruin our prey before she reaches him."

"The lake of sulfur!" the other swans chanted in unison. "He'll throw her into the lake of sulfur!"

A few of the swans spat at her. Others hissed in her face.

Margaret bit her lip hard and felt panic clutching her on the inside. She had not bargained for anything as hideous as this, nor had she ever supposed that even Regalia swans could be so bloodthirsty. They had her trapped now and there was no place to hide. The foulness of the air and the stifling heat made Margaret want to gag. The swans made a tight circle around her and began to waddle forward. Margaret had to move with them; she had no choice. She did not wish to be brutally pecked for making a struggle. Besides, even if she were to free herself, there was no place to go. The only way out of this Godforsaken place that she knew of was the way she had come in, and that had been a near vertical drop.

She looked at the swans surrounding her. Their empty faces were fixed straight ahead and their eyes stared out of their tiny sockets with unblinking resolve. It was useless to try to get Hector to recognize her. He hadn't even flinched when she called him by name. She wished she could be like Laurel and simply touch Hector and watch that glazed mist fall from his eyes. If only she hadn't left the others! If only Laurel were here! Then she remembered the magic feather. It was high time she used it before it was too late. Why had it taken her so long to think of it? Perhaps this stifling heat and sickening smell were beginning to hypnotize her as well.

They were approaching a narrow stone staircase, and the swans pushed her forward. The staircase was only wide enough for one, and they wanted Margaret to go first. Very slowly Margaret began to climb the steps. As inconspicuously as possible she unzipped her overall bib pocket.

"Move it!" one of the swans ordered.

Margaret felt a few painful pecks at her ankles and continued on a bit more quickly. Not that the swans were adept at stairs themselves. Margaret knew they were struggling up and over each one. She could hear them grunting and stumbling behind her. She had her hand in her pocket and her fingers clutched the magic feather. Maybe, just maybe, if she tried to race up the steps ahead of them she could get away. With a sudden bolt Margaret leapt up the staircase, taking two steps at a time and leaving her captors behind. She heard Hector yelling, "Get her back! Get her back!"

There was little the other swans could do. No one flew up after her; their wings had all been clipped.

The stone staircase curved up around to the left and then ended abruptly in front of an arched stone door that had an iron ring for a handle. There was nowhere else to go but through it and Margaret pulled on the ring. The door opened partway and she darted through. She found herself in a long dark corridor with flickering lanterns hanging at irregular intervals along the wall. They were casting odd-looking shadows on the ceiling and floor. Margaret had no idea where to go next. With her heart pounding heavily against her chest she began running as fast as she could down the hall to the right. Hurtling through the corridor she held the magic feather in front of her.

"Laurel!" she cried in desperation. "Laurel! Help me, Laurel!"

"Who goes there?" several voices in front of her chimed together in tinkly unison.

Margaret stopped dead in her tracks. Six, sleek white swans waddled toward her with silver whistles dangling from their slender necks. Their wings were long, not clipped short, and their feathers had an iridescent sheen to them even in the dimly lit corridor.

"We are the Leadership of the Regalia," a swan on the far left told her daintily, "and we forbid you to speak the name you just spoke on these premises. You are obviously with the Enemy. We must destroy you at once."

16

SEBASTIAN

Margaret turned around to run but it was no use. The swans from the Penance Room had made it to the top of the stairs and were bearing down on her from behind. She was trapped again. She felt her magic feather being jerked out of her hand. One of the six Leadership swans had it in his beak and the other five were staring at it.

"Just a common feather," one of them remarked. "Can't be anything worthwhile."

"We shall take it to the Great One just the same," said another. "Perhaps it has some sort of power attached to it."

Hector was drawing near now with a brisk waddle.

"Excuse me, sires," he said, bending his neck down low and addressing the Leadership. "With all due respect, sires, I am the one who found the creature. She came in of her own accord. Claims she came in through the Great One's passageway. It is my rightful duty to accompany her to the Great One myself and receive my reward for turning her in."

"Begone, Number 52!" one of the Leadership ordered him severely.

"You let her get away!" said another of the six. "We recovered her."

"You are the lowest in the pecking order. How dare you presume to lay eyes on the Great One!" said still another. "Back to the Penance Room where you belong. All of you! On the double."

"But sires . . ." objected Hector, but he never finished his sentence.

In a hissing rage the six swans opened their wings and flew at him with wild vengeance flaming in their eyes. Margaret backed up against the opposite wall and watched aghast as the Leadership began to fiercely peck and maul Hector until Margaret was sure he was quite dead. She wanted to stop them. She wanted to beat them off and rescue Hector again from their cruelty, but she knew there was nothing she could do. Instead she watched, plastered up against the wall, unmoving, her eyes wide with horror. At first Hector screamed terrible screams and struggled, flapping uselessly against his assailants. It seemed like forever that he struggled in vain against the relentless brutality. Finally, he went limp and fell silent in a bloody heap on the floor. Only then did the Leadership withdraw.

Margaret was paralyzed with fear. She had never seen anything so dreadful before. The other swans from the Penance Room looked on without so much as twitching a feather. Their empty faces displayed no emotion or sadness. To Margaret it seemed as if they had seen this type of assault many times before.

"Go!" commanded one of the Leadership to the Penance Room swans. "Go before you end up the same way! Let this be a lesson to you all. Never question the Leadership!"

In a flurry, the Penance Room swans turned and headed back down the corridor.

"I just don't understand it," said another of the Leadership in a dainty little voice, wiping the blood from his beak with his wing. "Why can't these swans understand the value of a pecking order and remember to obey without questioning? It really seems so simple."

"We are dealing with morons, Hillary," said another. "That is why they must be controlled. Otherwise we might be faced with total anarchy of the most barbaric kind. They are simply not a civilized lot like you and me."

"Right now we have this landbred creature to attend to," said the largest of the six. "It is high time we bring her to the throne room. Let the corpse lie there."

They surrounded Margaret and escorted her further down the hall. There was no way for Margaret to bolt this time. There were two swans flanking her on either side, a swan in front and a swan in back.

Hadn't Laurel heard her plea for help? Where was he? She had only been able to call his name a couple of times. What if it hadn't been enough? What if he hadn't heard her?

They led her through a series of padded double doors and finally came into a huge, dim room with white marble floors. Here the leadership stopped and bowed down low. Margaret didn't bow down. She wouldn't. She stood bolt upright, her arms folded across her chest. She hated this Regalia, and although she was more frightened than she had ever been before, her stubborn streak prevailed. She might be about ready to die, but she wasn't giving in to these horrid creatures for one second. Besides, at first she couldn't see anyone to bow down to, anyway.

Looking straight ahead, however, she did notice a few wide steps going up to a landing. Here, a white mist that seemed to come up out of the floor curled around itself like a well-charmed snake. She was overwhelmed again with the putrid sulfur smell that hung like rancid poison in the air. The heat was more dense even than the Penance Room. For a moment she felt as if she might faint. If only she could get to her canteen for some more water, but she knew she couldn't chance it. She didn't want to risk getting mauled like Hector and however many others who had gone before him. She stood stock-still and waited.

Finally, from out of the fog emerged a tall, lean swan. He was larger than any of the Leadership. Margaret would have said he was white, except for a dull greenish hue to his feathers that made him look like an old antique that needed polishing. His face was thin and his eyes skinny and long. When he saw Margaret his eyes seemed to pierce right through her like little jagged knives.

"Well, well," he mused casually, coming off the landing and walking down to them. "What have we here?"

His voice was thick and pasty and it had a familiar ring.

"Oh Great One!" exclaimed one of the Leadership swans. "We have found another landbred creature and we place it honorably at your disposal."

"And we have a feather, your Grace," one of them added. "It was found in the creature's grip."

"Throw it away!" the Great One remarked wearily. "Probably one of their religious superstitions."

He looked Margaret over disdainfully with a slight smirk forming around the corners of his beak.

"How quaint," he continued with a note of disgust in his voice. "Two featherless landbred scum arriving just minutes apart. Whatever shall we do with them?"

A raucous cackle escaped from the Leadership that sounded almost like laughter but was a bit too forced.

"I shall have no choice but to exterminate you immediately, my dear, with the other one," the Great One continued, as if speaking about the weather.

His eyes weren't glazed. They were just watery and red in the corners.

"You are not a credit to our cause, although I can't understand why you must oppose me. It is *I* who want to save your precious Joona, not destroy it. But what do you know? You have always opposed me, and finally I have you before me to do with as I please. How justified I feel! Of course I could make sport of it and kill you slowly. It would certainly humor me, but under the circumstances I think it safer if I do away with you quickly and not delay. You have a habit of consistently slipping away from me, and we wouldn't want that to happen again, now would we?"

Margaret stared transfixed at the tall, thin bird. The voice, the green hue, the loathsome familiarity this swan claimed to have with her all added up.

"Sebastian," Margaret rasped, for her throat was very dry. "It's you, isn't it?"

"Claim to recognize me, do you?" uttered the Great One irritably. "You see, that is the precise reason I must destroy you. You are much too outspoken. Do bring the other one to me," he added, addressing the Leadership with a vague motion of his left wing. "On the double, please."

Margaret couldn't stop trembling. Despite the oppressive heat, it felt like a cold clammy hand had hold of her heart and was mercilessly squeezing it dry. The six Leadership swans nodded. They waddled forward and disappeared into the sulfur mist swirling about the platform.

"It will be quite easy to do away with you," the Great One, who was really Sebastian, continued with an air of light-hearted satisfaction. "If you will notice, the mist of sulfur is actually coming up through a large opening in the floor. I had the opening carved out of the stone so the mist from the lake of sulfur in the Penance Room could reach me. I find the sulfur aroma appealing. It does wonders for my sinus condition, and I find it helps me sleep at night. I thought the opening in the floor would also be a wonderful way to dispose of unwanted material promptly. You and the other landbred creature will have the distinct honor of being the first of the enemy to be tossed into the lake of sulfur from this great height. Just a little push over the ledge of my lovely little venting system and we have an efficient completion to the process. Of course it won't be an actual completion. The lake of sulfur doesn't "kill" you as you might think. Rather, it causes you to writhe in torment. Once in, there is no way out, so you might as well consider yourself miserably dead. Scream as you may for mercy from its hot and angry depths, no one will rescue you. I thought it up myself."

Sebastian gave a heinous laugh that sent chills shuddering down Margaret's spine. Her life danced before her eyes in bits and snippets like multicolored lights. Uncle John, Laurel's face, her mother, Craig, Ryan, and Heather (where were they?), Clyde selling his stupid twizzlers, her friend Darcy, her school classroom, even Auntie Emily was in there somewhere shaking an index finger at her. She felt herself swaying and would have lost her balance and fallen had not the sight of Theodore emerging from the mist jolted her upright. He was escorted in by the swans. When he saw Margaret an immense grin spread across his wide, open face.

Despite their predicament, Margaret felt an intense relief at seeing him. He appeared so completely at ease. *Poor Theodore*, thought Margaret. *He doesn't understand what's happening*. She supposed it was for the better. They brought him to stand next to her, and Margaret grabbed his arm and hugged it.

"Oh Theodore! I'm so happy to see you!" she cried. "I wish you could tell me how you ended up in this horrible place!"

Theodore looked down at her and his grin seemed to grow even wider.

"Not right now," he told her softly. "I'm just glad to see you're okay. We were all so worried."

"Theodore!" Margaret shouted, her eyes growing wide.

"Enough!" commanded Sebastian with a thick, pasty drawl. "No more conversation!"

"Theodore!" Margaret declared again with complete astonishment. "You can talk!"

"Silence!" bellowed Sebastian in a rage. His eyes were flaming and the lime-green hue in his feathers grew brighter. "Take them to the ledge and throw them down! This lack of respect for authority will not be tolerated in my kingdom! On the double!"

The Leadership surrounded both of them and they began moving toward the platform.

"I guess this is it, Theodore," Margaret said, looking up at him.

Theodore just winked at her. "Keep your chin up," he advised gently.

They went up the stairs to the platform and stood side by side in a haze of sulfur. Margaret could barely breathe. She couldn't even see the opening in the floor. She couldn't see Sebastian and the other swans. All that was visible was cloud upon cloud of white churning mist.

"Now, my poor featherless dears, you are at the very edge of, shall we say, total and complete immersion in misery," Sebastian said sweetly from somewhere. "Do you wish to recite any last parting reflections on the meaninglessness of your pathetic existence (I do so love sentiment!), or should I simply give the word and have the Leadership throw you down?"

"What a jerk!" Margaret spat out angrily, loud enough for Sebastian to hear.

She heard Theodore chuckle. How on earth could he chuckle at a time like this?

"Very well then," Sebastian retorted mildly. "If you wish to spurn my generous offer we shall proceed. On the count of three, Leadership! You shall push them over. One . . . Two. . . ."

Margaret had closed her eyes tightly and was bracing herself. She had her arm linked through Theodore's. At least they were together. It was a selfish thought, but it greatly comforted her. Sebastian was supposed to say "Three!" Margaret waited but never heard it. Instead, another voice, which seemed much louder and very clear, cried, "Halt!"

17
LAUREL
COMES

The word was a loud command and seemed to be uttered by a member of the Regalia superior to Sebastian, although Margaret knew Sebastian had no superior. Unless.... Theodore pulled her away from the ledge. The Leadership, who had been clustered about them breathing down their necks, had drawn back as well. They had to be careful to go backwards the way they had come. They didn't want to risk falling in an opening they couldn't see.

"How did you get in here?" they heard Sebastian bellow.

Emerging from the mist, Margaret and Theodore saw him. Laurel stood in the center of the room. His wings were spread wide open, and his feathers were a brilliant white. He was so much larger than Sebastian. At least four times his size. Next to Laurel's brilliant white feathers, Sebastian appeared not only puny but much more green. Margaret gave a sigh and her whole body relaxed. Now everything was going to be all right. She raced over to Laurel and leaned her head against his chest. The depth of his wound was clearly visible just now. It was almost as if he were showing it to Sebastian to remind him of something.

"You called me, Margaret?" Laurel said, standing stock-still with his wings spread wide.

Laurel stared at Sebastian and his eyes were full of movement and light. Sebastian had retreated slightly but was still standing a few feet off looking glumly at the floor.

"Yes, Laurel," Margaret cried, hugging him. "Take me away from this place, Laurel."

Sebastian shot a look at both of them.

"That's not playing by the rules!" he said with an eerie singsong jeer. "And they're your rules, Laurel. I didn't set them."

"How did you get in here, Margaret?" Laurel asked, still unflinching, staring at Sebastian.

"She came of her own accord," one of the Leadership called out shakily. The six swans were standing behind Sebastian in a tight bunch looking terrified.

"Is that true, Margaret?" Laurel asked.

"Yes, yes it's true," Margaret confessed awkwardly. "I came in through the green door underneath the falls."

Margaret saw Sebastian grow fidgety. He flashed Margaret a withering look.

"You came through my secret chambers?" he spat at her. "No one can get in there. That door is always locked. You must be joking as only a pitiful landbred creature can joke. It isn't the least bit humorous, I might add."

"Your star, Margaret!" Theodore said. He was standing behind her and tapping her on the shoulder. "Do you have your star, Margaret?"

Margaret let go of Laurel and turned to face Theodore. She looked down. The star was hanging down behind her overall bib. She pulled it out. As she did so, she saw Sebastian cringe backwards and cover his face with his wing.

"Right of passage!" Theodore declared. "She has right of passage, Sebastian. Any place is open for her as she chooses."

Sebastian peered from behind his wing, eyeing Margaret warily.

"She's mine, I tell you!" he screamed at Laurel in a high-pitched panic. "She came in here of her own accord. The other one was captured. Take him and go, but leave her here."

Sebastian slowly let his wing down. He seemed confused and anxiously moved his head about to the right and to the left. Then a kind of wild, relieved look crept into his eyes.

"She doesn't know!" he pealed out suddenly. "The creature hasn't a clue! How perfectly like you, Laurel, to imbue such ignorant beings with weapons they don't even know how to use. Afraid they'll overtake you, huh? Run you out of business? A kind of perverted humor, if you ask me! Maybe we're more alike than you think."

"Silence!" Laurel demanded. He still hadn't moved from his original stance. "I wish to make a proposal, Sebastian, and I wish to do it now. The rules stand firm. Margaret is rightfully yours, for as you have stated she entered this domain of her own accord."

Margaret's face fell. She couldn't believe her ears.

"But I didn't know!" she cried. "I didn't know what I was doing!"

Laurel relaxed his posture. He folded one wing and put the other up around Margaret's shoulders. He nuzzled her cheek gently with his downy-soft head. Then he slowly turned his gaze toward Sebastian who was eyeing Laurel suspiciously. A greenish gleam crept into his eyes.

"Well then, we do agree," Sebastian said slyly. "Ever since the beginning Joona has been under your law—your strange law of free will, which I never understood. Your strange law that clearly states that should a creature willfully leave your paradise and venture into my domain they are my rightful property to do with as I please. I am glad we see eye to eye on this matter, for should you contend with the law we all know what that would mean for your little paradise."

Laurel turned toward Margaret.

"Should I counter the law on which Joona was founded, the rainbow would cease to shine. I cannot take you from him, Margaret. It would destroy Joona to break a law so fundamental to its founding. Joona was made for freedom. Freedom of movement, of choice, of expression. To forcefully work against the law of freedom would bring utter destruction to this land."

"Oh Laurel!" Margaret cried, clutching at the swan's feathery chest. "Don't leave me here! Please help me! I didn't know what choice I was making when I entered this horrible place!"

Margaret's voice went dry. Her heart was pounding. She could hear each throb as if it were a drum beating out the seconds of her life.

"So now," Sebastian ordered, approaching Margaret stealthily, "hand over the creature. She belongs to me."

"I myself will go in her place," Laurel told Sebastian quietly, "if I have your word that you will release them both. It's within the law's capacity to allow for a substitution."

Margaret's mouth dropped open and she felt her gooseflesh crawling.

"What are you saying?" she demanded, still clutching at Laurel's feathery chest. "No Laurel! No! You can't do this."

A sob caught in her throat and her eyes were brimming. She looked at Sebastian. The greenish gleam in his eyes glittered at her like cheap sequins.

"A wonderful trade!" Sebastian declared agreeably. "Quite an appropriate proposal I must say, since you're the one who is responsible for your careless, ignorant followers bumbling into my castle unannounced and bringing chaos to my well-ordered, well-supervised kingdom."

"Do I have your word on their release?" Laurel asked him simply.

"My word? Certainly," Sebastian said in a low voice. "What are they in comparison to you?"

Margaret, still clutching at Laurel's chest, buried her face in his sweet-smelling feathers.

"No!" she sobbed. "You can't go. I won't let you!"

"Leadership!" Sebastian ordered. "Take him to the ledge."

The six swans scurried over. Margaret felt Theodore's hands on her shoulders, pulling her away from Laurel. Margaret struggled, but Theodore held her firmly.

"It must be this way," Theodore spoke softly in her ear. "You mustn't stop him."

The Leadership surrounded Laurel and escorted him away.

"You don't need to escort me. Or force me. I am willing to go on my own," Laurel told them in a quiet, steady voice, but no one listened.

They brought him up the platform steps and disappeared with him into the sinister mist.

"On the count of three!" Sebastian declared with obvious elation. "One . . . two . . . three!"

Margaret heard it even though she couldn't see it—the six swans shuffling forward to push Laurel in and the dull far-away splash moments later as Laurel plunged into the lake. Then there was heavy silence like the kind that happens after someone has shared dreadful news with someone else. The Leadership emerged out of the swirling mist; Laurel was gone. Just then Sebastian screamed a high-pitched yowl that rose and fell like laughter twisted with hatred.

"It's mine!" he cried, lifting his wings and moving about in a contorted type of dance. "Joona is mine! Leadership! On the double! Throw these wretches in with him and take from the weak one her silver star!"

"Run, Margaret, run!" Theodore cried, pushing her forward. "Don't let them have it, Margaret. It mustn't fall into the hands of the enemy!" Margaret trembled and her eyes were blinded by tears, but she stumbled forward. She didn't understand what difference the star made now that Laurel was dead. Joona, the paradise for suffering swans, was no more. When she got to the double padded doors, Sebastian was there to meet her. His feathers were almost completely green now.

"There is no escaping me, you wretch," he sneered. "Don't be naive. You are nothing without him. Nothing! Now give me the star!"

"You gave your word you would let me go!" Margaret screamed at him, holding the star to her chest with both hands. "I will never give you my star. *Never!*"

She began to back up slowly. She heard a commotion behind her. Theodore was struggling with the Leadership. The six swans were not to be deterred. They hissed and pecked at Theodore until he lost his balance and fell to the floor with a thud. Then the Leadership surrounded Margaret, waiting for their orders.

"Yes, you and your friend Laurel are very naive," Sebastian said, slowly coming toward her. "What was to prevent me from killing you after your precious Laurel had left the scene, may I ask you? Did you trust me? Trust is never wise. It is better to distrust everything and everyone all the time. How do you think I made it where I am now? But not that you care. You are too contaminated with the Enemy's queer, illogical ideas about things that don't exist anymore, like truth and justice. It is those archaic ideas that keep us all in check and limit Joona's progress and efficient management of space. You have nowhere to hide and no place to go. No one is fighting for you now. You might as well hand over the star or I will order the Leadership to attack."

Margaret clutched the star and looked desperately for a place to run. She was surrounded. She looked over at Theodore. He was just getting up off the floor and had blood on his shirt. Sebastian was right. She was alone.

18
THE RESCUE

Suddenly, like a splash of sunlight bursting through the clouds on a dreary day, the double padded doors behind Sebastian blew open and a wonderfully cool breeze swirled into the sticky room. Margaret's hair blew back from her face and she saw a white swan with an orange beak flying directly toward her. The swan passed her and dove at the Leadership, who scattered in all directions. There was someone riding on the swan's back, but the swan was moving too fast for Margaret to tell who it was. Then came a flash of white light like lightning. It came in little bursts and seemed to emanate from the swan himself. Theodore was at Margaret's side now and moved her against the wall.

"Don't get in the way of the beams," he told her. "But don't worry; we are safe now. It's Heather and Alexander. Heather's star is blinding them, Margaret. You see, it's not only for right of passage; it's also a weapon. I couldn't tell you before. I didn't want the Regalia to know how to use it. They know it's dangerous, but how to use it is a secret that's been preserved for eons. Should they gain possession of a star and learn its secret it would mean disaster."

Margaret stared at him. He would have died and let her

die in order to preserve the star's secret. She couldn't fathom such loyalty. Theodore's shirt was wet with blood.

"Are you all right?" she asked him.

Theodore gave a wave of his hand.

"Just a few nicks here and there. Nothing a little Joona water won't wash away."

The room was in an uproar. Margaret could see the long white beams now, flashing like swords of lightning. When a beam hit one of the swans they would fall backwards like a corpse. Gradually the swans would revive, but without eyesight. Four swans who had been hit already and revived, walked aimlessly about in circles. Two of them were still on the loose, running around with their beaks wide open in fright.

"Let me show you how the star works, Margaret."

Theodore held Margaret's star, took Joona water from her canteen, and rubbed it on the surface. Then he showed her how to aim and fire. Margaret watched him amazed, and taking the star in hand she tried a few shots herself. Meanwhile, Heather and Alexander hit the last two swans and landed breathlessly in front of Margaret and Theodore.

"The castle's under siege!" Heather told them. "And there are more swans that need to be dealt with. Craig is in the Penance Room. I'm off to help him. Laurel's swans are taking over the posts of the Regalia. Oh Margaret! I'm so glad you're all right."

"I wouldn't be, if it wasn't for you," Margaret told her. "You saved my life. Another second and I would have been dead meat. I'm grateful to you."

She looked at Heather astride Alexander. Heather looked so different. Her pale cheeks were rosy and her usually neat, perfect hair was flying out in every direction. Most striking to Margaret was the light in her eyes. She looked young, vibrant, and more beautiful than Margaret could ever remember.

"Thank goodness we got here in time," Heather replied,

shaking her head. "You can thank a swan named Priscilla for that. She told me you might have been taken here. We're going to have an easy victory, Margaret. Joona will be a paradise again. You wait and see! But I've got to go. The others will be needing assistance."

"Later!" Alexander called out.

They took off and flew hastily out of the room. Margaret looked around and saw the six Leadership swans waddling aimlessly about, croaking out desperate pleas for help.

"What's to become of them?" she asked Theodore. "I almost feel sorry for them."

"Let them be for now," Theodore told her. "We must be off as well to join in the attack. We will go on foot and search the corridors and stairways. You must use your star on any of the enemy you see and I will help you spot them."

"What about Sebastian?" Margaret asked. "I don't see Sebastian."

"Sebastian is a coward," Theodore said with a smirk. "At times like this he never fights. He retreats into his shadowy caves and waits to emerge at a better time. He never stands behind his followers. He cares nothing for them."

"I couldn't tell Heather about Laurel," Margaret said, looking down. "She was so happy."

"I understand," Theodore said softly, looking at her with large, sorrowful eyes. "I understand."

They searched the corridors and stairways for at least three hours. There were more nooks and crannies to the castle than Margaret ever dreamed possible. They found at least half a dozen swans hiding under the steps and a few more in closets and behind tapestries. Others were out guarding the front, oblivious to the attack going on inside.

Each time Margaret used her star she felt an odd mixture of emotions. Even though she was glad she was no longer defenseless and at the mercy of the Regalia, she still felt a pang of guilt. The Regalia swans, who had looked so fearsome before, now looked pitiable and weak. They cowered and cried out for mercy, but Theodore was firm. They were meant to use the stars on the enemy and there could be no compromise. He told Margaret that Milohe meant it to happen this way, otherwise he wouldn't have equipped her with a star. Margaret knew he was probably right. She remembered what the sacred text said about everyone fighting with commitment and resolve, and she complied. After all, it wasn't like she was killing them, although blinding them to her seemed almost worse.

Finally, after they were convinced they had searched and found the remainder of the Regalia, they made their way to the Penance Room. The other three had done their work well. The swans who had been prisoners were gathered around Craig, Ryan, and Heather whooping it up, while the Regalia, stone-blind, were either sitting motionless or wandering around bumping into things and calling for help.

"Margaret! Theodore!" cried Ryan when he saw them.

He made his way through the band of happy swans with Craig and Heather at his heels. He embraced Margaret, then Theodore, and stood there grinning.

"Gee whiz, I guess we showed them!" he declared, putting his hands on his hips. "We just finished. There were tons of Regalia to be shot."

"Thanks for the water, Margaret," shouted a large swan. "Couldn't have lasted a moment longer without it!"

"Samson!"

Margaret ran over and kissed him on the top of his head.

"Samson, I was so worried about you."

"Wait until Laurel sees what a great job we did!" sputtered Craig. "He'll be so proud of us!"

Margaret looked down and dug her toe into the sand.

"Why do you look so glum, Margaret?" Heather asked, coming over to her. "Are you sick?"

Margaret just stood slouched over and stared at her feet. "Did they hurt you up there?" Heather persisted.

"No," said Margaret lowly. "It's . . . it's Laurel. They threw him into the lake of sulfur. Didn't any of you down here see him falling in?"

"We saw something awfully big splash down and go under," one of the swans recalled. "But we didn't think it was him. No sir. Never Laurel. Not in a million years."

"Well it was him," Margaret told them soberly. "He went in my place."

The happy party was over. A hush settled over the little band of celebrants and everyone found a place on the ground to sit down. It was desperately hot and rancid in the Penance Room, but no one seemed to notice now. Their victory had been short-lived and everything they had done completely pointless. Laurel was their Champion, their Hope, their Guide. Without him the battle was lost, not won. Margaret didn't know how long they sat in the oppressive heat staring into the sulfuric mist as the cries of the blind, wandering Regalia swans filled the air. It seemed like forever. It seemed like hell. "He was so kind to me," Heather said finally, wiping away a tear. "I didn't think anything could ever destroy him."

"I hate to say it," Craig said after another very long pause. "But has anyone given any thought to how we're supposed to get out of here? I mean, without Laurel around we're basically stranded in Joona."

"I'm in no hurry," Heather said and sniffed. "Nothing matters anymore anyway. I'd just like to get out of this hateful room. It's hotter than blazes in here."

"It's just like you, Craig," Ryan said with an exasperated sigh, "to think only of yourself in a time of crisis."

Alexander stepped forward.

"In answer to Craig's question, I am afraid to say there is no way out of Joona without Laurel. The rest of us are not

148

permitted to enter earth's zone. If we do, we cannot return. If that were not the case, four of us stronger swans could give each of you a lift. As it is, your return back to earth presents a dilemma for us all."

"Maybe we could live here," Ryan suggested halfheartedly. "Although, without Laurel, who knows what this place will become?"

"Laurel isn't finished with us yet," Margaret blurted out. "He can't be!"

Everyone stared at her. Margaret had no idea where her words had come from, and she didn't know what they meant. They had just come, unplanned, out of her mouth without any effort on her part.

"Besides," she continued, trying to sound logical lest the others think she had gone insane, "we can't just leave these poor, blind swans here. They'll die of confusion and starvation. We must see if we can help them."

Theodore nodded. Craig looked exasperated.

"Margaret!" he exclaimed. "We can't help them. There's nothing we can do, especially without Laurel. Besides, we're not supposed to care about them. They're the enemy."

"Well, I care," Margaret replied testily. "Even if I'm not supposed to. Perhaps we could just go around and try to make them a bit more comfortable. Maybe bring them something to eat."

"Watch it! Stop getting me wet!" one of the swans yelled to another swan standing behind him. "That water is hot!"

"I didn't do anything," the other swan retorted. "I just got doused myself."

"Hey look!" Priscilla cried. "The water in the sulfur lake. It's rising!"

They all looked. Indeed, the lake was rising in a most peculiar fashion. The water in the center was coming together to form a mountainous wave that stood at least twelve feet above the surface. The rest of the water on the sides splashed outward and up onto anyone who was within range. It was breathtaking to watch.

At one point all of them got a little wet when an extra large wave sloshed its way over the bank. The water was terribly hot and everyone cried out when they were hit. It left a terrible stench on feathers and skin.

The mist was thinning now, dispersed by the movement of the water, and everyone could see what was happening in the middle of the lake.

"Run for your lives!" one of the swans shouted. "The mountain in the middle looks like it's going to explode."

Several of the swans retreated hastily. Others just stood and stared. It did appear that the mountain of water was about to erupt. It convulsed violently as if it were full of something it simply could not contain. Then the peak of the mountain curled open, much the way the petals of a flower open on a spring morning. Little waves and rivulets flipped over and bounced down the trembling inclines from the summit. There was a sputtering and gurgling.

Margaret could see bits of water and seaweed spewing out of the top as if someone were doing spring cleaning and tossing out old junk that had been collecting for too long. Suddenly, like a shot exploding from a cannon, something brilliantly white burst forth from the peak. It looked like a bolt of white lightning, much like the beams from the stars, except it was much larger. It soared upward to the ceiling and then circled around again and again like a meteor in orbit. It had a head and a tail and was making a rhythmic "shush" as it sped in circles up over their heads.

"It's Laurel!" Margaret cried. "He's come back!"

"Watch out!" Heather yelled. "The mountain! It's collapsing!"

19
THE
RESTORATION

Margaret, who was closest to the edge, was hit first and bowled off her feet. She expected to be terribly burned. Instead she found herself washed over with water that was refreshing and cool. It made her tingle the way Joona water did. As the wave subsided she looked about her. Heather, Ryan, and Craig were half-sitting, half-lying on the ground, drenched from head to foot. The swans looked nonplussed, having simply floated on the wave. Margaret took a deep breath. Something was different. Quite different.

Then she knew. The smell! The rancid sulfur smell was gone and in its place was the alluring aroma of pine and lilac. Glancing at the lake she saw that the mist had completely evaporated. The mountain had subsided and the water was still, with hardly a ripple on the surface. She crawled to the edge of the bank and peered in. Her reflection was as clear as if she were looking into the finest glass mirror. She almost laughed outright when she saw herself. Her bangs were plastered on her forehead in wads, and her braids, hanging down over her shoulders, dripped at the tips. Heather crawled up next to her and peered into the water. Her hair was disheveled and dripping too.

"Wow!" she said, surveying herself critically. "You never imagine yourself the way you actually look. Why didn't you tell me my hair looked . . . oh, who cares?"

"Where's Laurel?" Margaret asked, looking up at the ceiling.

The bright white meteor was gone.

"I dunno, Margaret," Heather said, still gazing at her reflection. "Are you sure what came shooting out of the top was Laurel?"

"Greetings," said a spirited voice behind them.

They saw his reflection in the water first. Laurel had come up between them, silently, and they hadn't even noticed. They turned and embraced him, Heather on one side, Margaret on the other, and buried their faces in his feathers while the others ran over to join them.

"Laurel!" Margaret cried. "I thought you were never coming back!"

"I always come back," Laurel said with jubilance. "Always."

"But the lake of sulfur," Margaret managed, blinking back tears of joy. "It's a place of torment forever. No one is ever supposed to return."

Laurel looked them over. First Margaret, then Heather, then Ryan and Craig. Finally he looked at Theodore and the swans. There was intense joy in his eyes and a brilliance about his countenance that made it difficult to look directly at him for very long.

"There is now no more lake of sulfur," Laurel announced regally. "For sulfur is not fit for swans to play in. It has been purified for you. Only Joona water fills the great lake now."

"Did it hurt?" Theodore asked, crouching down to the swan's level. "Tell us what happened."

"You will never know exactly what happened," Laurel replied, looking back at Theodore with such brilliance in his face that Theodore had to drop his eyes to the ground. "I would not wish you to know the extent of the pain, nor do I expect you to bear it. It is not for you to know. And yet, I knew that if I descended low enough, all the way down through that murky darkness, Milohe would be there to take me in."

"So you knew all the time?" Craig asked. "You knew you would be okay?"

Laurel sighed and his sigh was almost a groan.

"I knew Milohe would be there, Craig," Laurel replied slowly. "He's always at the beginning and end of every road. He is, in fact, the road itself, although He's sometimes hard to recognize. The thing I didn't know was if I could make it all the way down to the very bottom of the lake without losing my direction. It was dark and chaotic and the water burned me.

"It is written in the sacred text that if one swan were able to endure it, descending all the way down into a place of great evil and emerging from it unscathed, he would bring purification. Milohe was at the bottom of the lake to comfort me when I got there. Otherwise I would have become disoriented. He gave me strength to resurface again and pointed me upward. Remember this, children. No matter how deep the pit, Milohe goes deeper still. That is the message from the sacred text, and it is true. I have proven it to you."

Margaret wept unabashedly. She rested her head against Laurel's smooth, soft back and stroked him gently.

"It was all because of me," she sobbed. "It was a big mistake. If I hadn't gone off and. . . ."

"My dear Margaret," Laurel interrupted gently, nuzzling her with his beak. "The way things happen has been written down ahead of time in the sacred text. There are no mistakes. To be a part of the story itself, that is the only choice. I am glad you are part of my story. Very glad."

The air was cool now and the fragrance of pine and lilac filled the air with the freshness of springtime. Some of the

swans waddled over to the still, clear lake, and after surveying it curiously, plunged in for a dip. Theodore followed with
a great grand dive, and Craig cannonballed in after him. Ryan,
Margaret, and Heather stayed next to Laurel for a moment
longer.

"There is one more thing I must do," Laurel told them,
"before I take you home, although the hour is late."

"What is that?" Ryan asked.

"The Regalia can be healed," Laurel told them, compassion flooding his dark eyes. "As long as they admit they are
blind. It is a curious thing with some. The stars are meant to
bring the lost to their senses and convince them of their need.
Yet, even after they are blinded by the stars, some still refuse
my help. In that case, there is nothing I can do. I must go to
them now and see if they will receive me. I know them all by
name, for they were all mine once in the beginning."

They watched as Laurel waddled away from them a few
paces and approached the first blind swan. The swan was sitting statuelike on the ground, its motionless eyes staring
straight ahead at nothing. Laurel bent down low and said
something in the swan's ear. The swan nodded eagerly. Laurel
swept his long white wing over the top of the swan's head. The
swan shook himself and blinked his eyes several times in
succession.

"I can see!" the swan suddenly screamed out. "Hey! Hey!
You guys! I can see again. And . . . oh Laurel! I feel myself for
the first time in I don't know how long. I can think! I can feel!
I can see! I'm me! And my wings . . . Laurel, my wings! They're
long again and I can fly."

"It's wonderful to see you again, Constantine!" Laurel said,
bending down low in a swan smile.

Constantine's unrestrained jubilance was catching. It
didn't take long for a crowd of the blind to gather around
Laurel. Constantine soared about the Penance Room, send-

ing others to Laurel by twos and threes. Soon the room was filled with shouts and loud trumpeting as swans who had been healed began to celebrate. Some of them plunged into the water and chased each other in circles. Others took to the air and coasted round and round the room, diving and crossing each other at all kinds of precarious angles. The splashing and soaring and carrying on was so great that Margaret could scarcely hear herself when she spoke to Ryan and Heather.

"We've got to go get Hector."

"What are you talking about, Margaret?" Ryan shouted back at her. "I think any swan who hasn't found his way down here by now with all this racket must be pretty dense!"

"Follow me."

She led them up the narrow staircase. The shadows cast by the flickering lanterns along the wall looked warm and comforting now. Margaret hoped beyond hope that Hector was still alive. She turned to the right and led Heather and Ryan down the corridor to a limp, lifeless mound of feathers that lay against the wall.

"He's dead," Ryan pronounced solemnly, when they reached him.

"Poor thing," Heather breathed, crouching down to get a closer look. "It looks like he bled to death."

"I want to bring him to Laurel anyway," Margaret decided. "Maybe he can still do something."

The three of them picked up the carcass gently. Hector's neck and head fell over and Margaret had to prop it up against her shoulder. The swan's eyes were closed and his beak was clamped shut over his protruding black tongue. The carcass was heavy, but not nearly as heavy as Alexander had been and there were three of them to carry it now.

Slowly they made their way back to the Penance Room. Laurel was surrounded by a crowd of swans so large that it was impossible to even get near. He was whispering something into a large, sleek swan's ear now. Margaret recognized the swan as one of the Leadership. To her absolute amazement the swan shook its head vehemently, and waddled off still blinded. The swan was in a fury, cackling angrily to itself. So incensed was the swan that it actually tripped over its own feet and landed with a belly flop on the ground.

Margaret, Ryan, and Heather put Hector carefully down and walked over.

"Can we help you?" Heather asked the swan.

The swan's eyes were like stones staring up at them, seeing nothing.

"Of course not!" the swan retorted angrily, fumbling around a bit. He sniffed and snorted and then managed to get back on his feet. "I don't need help from anyone. Can't you see that? I am perfectly fine the way I am and I resent the offer. In fact, it offends me! How dare you assume to offer help to one of the Leadership?"

"How strange," Heather mused, as they walked back to Hector. "How very strange that he wouldn't know he was blind."

They waited a long time for the crowd to disperse around Laurel. It wasn't simply those who needed healing that surrounded him. It was also those who were celebrating. Some of the swans were just following Laurel from sheer gratitude that he had given them back their sight and with it their sanity. The children might have waited forever had not Laurel looked at them. His eyes were brilliant, and he came over at once with his grand escort of jubilant swans following.

"Whatever do we have here?" he asked the children softly, pushing at the carcass with his beak. They could barely hear him because of the commotion in the room.

"I'm sorry to bother you, Laurel," Margaret said loudly. "But I thought just maybe you could do something."

"Why, it's Hector," Laurel said, looking at the swan's face with deep pity. "Oh Hector, take heart. It's all forgiven. Bring water, children. Bring lots of water. He's been dead for a while."

They ran and filled canteens with lake water. The room began to quiet down as the other swans stopped their clamor and came over to watch. Craig and Theodore came out of the lake and helped. At Laurel's instruction they poured water over the bird's head and body until he was drenched. Then Margaret and Theodore pried open Hector's beak, bent his head back, and poured water, as much as would go down, into his throat. Nothing happened. Hector lay there, his feathers drenched and plastered against his scrawny body, still and cold, like a lump of wet modeling clay.

"It's no use," Margaret sighed. "I'm sorry I bothered you, Laurel."

"Stand back," Laurel instructed, and the crowd moved backwards a few feet. Then Laurel opened his beak wide and breathed into Hector's face. Laurel's breath was fragrant and sweet and intensified the aroma of pine and lilac that was already in the room. It was more like a wind that Laurel breathed, for it was so powerful that it whipped Heather's hair around her face and blew Margaret's soggy bangs away from her forehead. The swans' feathers rippled in it and even the still, clear water in the lake wrinkled away from them in shiny silver streaks.

"Arise!" Laurel commanded the carcass as the wind from his breath still whispered round the room.

Hector's body flinched. Then it jumped. Hector began to cough and sputter and then he opened his eyes. The first thing he saw was Laurel standing with his head cocked to one side watching him. Then Hector stood up awkwardly, shook himself, and gazed around bewildered at the company of wide-eyed swans and children who were staring at him.

157

"Well, I'll be," Hector commented. "It must be my birthday or some such holiday. I've never had so many guests."

A cheer went up from the swans and Laurel bent down low in a swan smile.

"You were dead!" Margaret cried. "And now you are alive again."

Hector looked completely taken aback. Then as if remembering something, his brow furrowed.

"I believe you're right," he said pensively. "I believe I was in captivity, perhaps even here, in this very room. I wasn't . . . I couldn't have been part of the enemy's camp? They didn't capture me again, did they, Laurel? And make me one of them?"

Laurel nodded slowly.

"Oh!" Hector cried, and flung himself down at Laurel's feet, covering his face with his wings. "How could I have become their slave again? Can you ever forgive me? I'm sorry. So sorry. I didn't know what I was doing."

Hector began to bawl with heavy heaving sighs.

"Of course you didn't," Laurel said, speaking to him as a mother comforting a small child. "That is why I'm here to help you. Do get up now, Hector. All is forgiven. You have been miserable far too long. It is time to learn to laugh again."

Hector rose slowly to his feet, sniffing profusely and blinking his tiny brown eyes to keep back the tears. His eyes had lost their glaze and were warm and sparkling again.

"Because of you, Laurel," he rasped hoarsely. "Because of you, I will learn to laugh again."

Heather tapped Margaret on the shoulder.

"Look, Margaret!" she whispered. "Behind you! There's a beautiful woman over there. She just came down the staircase and she's motioning to you."

Margaret turned around. Standing at the bottom of the staircase was a woman dressed in white with a gold band of richly embroidered jewels wrapped loosely about her head.

She was smiling, and her long brown hair cascading down around her shoulders reminded Margaret of the waterfall in the cave. She recognized the woman at once. It was her mother.

"The queen!" one of the swans uttered, and everyone scrambled to their feet.

Margaret burst into a headlong sprint toward her.

"Margaret," her mother said softly, putting her arms out in welcome. "How my arms have ached to hold you."

Margaret flung herself into her mother's arms and the two of them embraced for a long time. She buried her face in her mother's robe and smelled the rich aroma of lilac and pine. Finally her mother pulled her away and gazed deeply into her eyes.

"You look well, my dear. You look very well, and I've yearned to see you for so long. Come, follow me, Margaret. I have much to tell you."

The queen smiled and Margaret followed her slowly up the narrow staircase.

"She's beautiful," whispered Priscilla. "I had no idea she was Margaret's mother. That makes Margaret a princess. We have been in the presence of royalty and not known it!"

Before they disappeared around the curve in the staircase Margaret turned and waved at them all. Everyone waved back. It was clear that the two of them did not wish to be disturbed for a while, and everyone understood.

20

GOING HOME

Try as she might, Margaret could never remember specifically what she and her mother discussed. Margaret thought when she returned to the others that it had been a couple of days, but those who were waiting for Margaret said she was gone for scarcely an hour. *Perhaps,* thought Margaret later, *it was the same way with her mother as it had been when Laurel went into Milohe.* Perhaps time in one place in Joona was not equal to the same amount of time in another place. Perhaps it was because when you were with someone you loved, time couldn't measure the intensity of it and just gave up trying.

After it was over, Margaret only remembered general things about her visit. Her mother had taken her to a large living room with wonderful couches that sank way down when you sat on them. A silver tray on the coffee table in front of them was full of delightful treats. Margaret remembered that she had eaten three vanilla cakes, two strawberry tarts, several handfuls of tiny mints, and hot chocolate. They had sat on one of the couches side by side talking about beautiful things that filled Margaret's heart to the brim with a wonderful warmth. She could only compare the experience to times when she had dreamt a great dream and awoke feeling marvelous but couldn't quite remember the details of what it was all about. She did know that her mother had told her some enchanting stories and given her some important messages. She couldn't recall exactly what the messages were, but she had the sense they were tucked deep inside her somewhere waiting to come out at just the right time. She did remember that her mother had told her she had been very brave when she encountered the Regalia and that her efforts had saved Joona from certain extinction. She had also told Margaret time and time again how much she loved her. It had been a grand comfort to know those things. It made Margaret feel all light and bubbly. Finally her mother had given her something to take back with her.

"Here," she had said, reaching into her pocket and pulling out an object she carefully placed in Margaret's hand. "This stone is for your uncle, Margaret. He and I were in Joona together on several occasions when we were children. We helped Laurel build this castle, and when we got to the throne room we built the marble platform out of smooth white stones. Your uncle was fascinated by these stones then, for he loved collecting rocks when he was a boy. He swore these were the most beautiful stones he had ever laid eyes on. In fact, to get them we had to dive off the shore of one of the islands and swim to the bottom of the lake. There were myriads upon myriads of white stones there, shining in the glistening water. We would lug them ashore in big nets and haul them to the castle with the help of the swans. Your uncle will remember it all when you give him the stone. It will help him to know that I am alive."

Margaret fingered the stone. It was a white, smooth, marble stone that shone like a polished pearl.

"It's beautiful," Margaret whispered. She put it carefully

into her overall bib pocket. "Tell me more about your adventures in Joona, Mother, when you were little."

She was sure her mother told her all about it, but she couldn't remember anything else except that when it was time to go she hadn't wanted to leave. Her mother told her gently that she must or she would be terribly late for earth. She had promised to see Margaret again and assured Margaret once again of her love. That was all.

The next thing she knew, Margaret found herself walking down the steps to the Penance Room. When she reached the room the sweet smell of pine and lilac wafted toward her. The air was cool and fresh. She saw that many of the swans were gathered around Ryan, Craig, Heather, and Theodore in a big circle. Laurel was talking with some other swans off to one side. It appeared that all of the swans who were still in the Penance Room had been healed of their blindness. As Margaret drew near, the swans who were sitting down around the children scrambled to their feet. Heather, Craig, Ryan, and Theodore also rose.

"We must rise in the presence of a princess," Priscilla cackled. "We had no idea you were . . . uh, royalty, Margaret. We hope your visit with her Majesty was a pleasant one."

"It was wonderful," Margaret said softly. "But please, all of you, sit down! I'm just Margaret and that's the way I want to stay."

"No! No!" Hector protested. "You must receive high honor for being the daughter of our queen. Samson! Fetch the wreath!"

Margaret started.

"What wreath?" she asked. "What are all of you up to?"

"The wreath of grape vines," said Alexander. "While you were gone, we made it for you. The vines from which your wreath is made at one time grew over the arched doorway that leads to Milohe himself. That is the doorway Laurel went through to get your stars, remember?"

"Of course I remember," said Margaret. "I could never forget."

"Occasionally," continued Alexander, "when the vines grow too long over the archway, one of us is summoned to prune them. The sacred remains are then brought to the castle. Some of them can be cut and planted in the royal gardens. The grapes that grow off of these branches are sweeter than honey and more succulent than wine. It is from these sacred remains that we have made your wreath, Margaret."

"But whatever for?" Margaret exclaimed.

The swans were standing about with radiant expressions on their faces. Ryan, Heather, Craig, and Theodore were grinning at her proudly.

"It is an honor, Margaret," Laurel said, coming forward. "The greatest honor the swans can give to you. By giving you the wreath they are choosing you to be their princess. It is one thing to be a princess because you are the daughter of our Queen. It is quite another thing to be a princess by popular demand. You will be both."

Samson waddled up to Laurel with the wreath of dark brown vines hanging from his beak.

"Margaret!" Laurel instructed her gently. "Please kneel at the water's edge."

Margaret knelt on the sandy bank beside the still waters of the lake. She looked up and saw Laurel's rich, dark eyes gazing down at her. The other swans watched her with eager expectation. The moment was magical. Margaret could not believe what was happening. Laurel rested the tip of his right wing on her head.

"I pronounce Margaret princess of Joona," Laurel declared. "And as these vines have come from Milohe's eternal domain, so may her reign in Joona be eternally peaceful, filled with light and music."

"But Laurel," Margaret objected, "I thought I had to go home."

"When you return to Joona, my child," Laurel told her softly. "Then you will reign with the queen."

"When will that be?" Margaret blurted out.

"It is not for us to know the time or the season, Margaret," Laurel said patiently. "But it shall happen. When you return, you shall wear this wreath of grape vines always as a sign of your royalty. For now, I will place it on your head momentarily as a sign that you are princess. You must then take it off and leave it here in Joona. We will keep it safe for you until your return."

Laurel took the wreath from Samson and placed it delicately on Margaret's head. It fit perfectly. A shudder ran down Margaret's spine. It was as if it were meant to be. Suddenly Margaret heard music. It was Joona music, the same music she had heard on her first journey here. Finally! Her heart jumped at the sound of it. She had missed this music with all her heart. She could listen to it forever.

The symphony of sound floated around her so close she felt as if she could touch it. It was electric and alive. Margaret wished she could capture it and take it home with her. The beauty of it fed her soul like water on a hot, humid day. The swans began to sing along, and their voices echoed off the stone walls of the Penance Room in rich, sweeping harmony. The words were familiar. Margaret remembered them. She looked over at Ryan and Craig. They nodded, remembering the words also.

"How beautiful the rainbow, whose light reverses death!
How beautiful the great white swan whose death became
     our life!
How wonderful the children who led us out of fright!

As long as we live, we will thank you! Thank you!
Thank you!"

The melody continued on, swirling about them with full-bodied resonance. Then Margaret heard Laurel's voice bouncing out joyfully over the swelling symphony of sound.

"Children! It's time to go. I must take you back now, for time is slipping away on earth and I am afraid we are very late. Come now! Hurry! Climb aboard."

"Must we?" Heather moaned. "Things are just starting to perk up around here. This music . . . it's . . . it's beautiful."

"Indeed!" Laurel declared with a cheerful lilt. "All of you did a wonderful job. What was to be accomplished has been accomplished. You have brought the music back to Joona, for now there is no more fear. Don't despair. I will meet with you again. Remember that. Until then, carry Joona in your heart. Earth longs for Joona music too, and you must bring it there as well."

"I will stay, Laurel," Theodore said, coming forward. "Until you return to watch over them."

Laurel nodded gratefully. The children reluctantly crawled up Laurel's wing and onto his back. Craig went first. Then Ryan and Heather. Margaret took her crown off and handed it to Alexander. Then she too climbed up Laurel's wing and settled in. It was hard to say goodbye to the swans. Margaret could see tears in some of their eyes. Her own eyes were misty as well. It was hard to leave the beautiful music, the peaceful quiet waters, the fragrance of lilac and pine. In her heart Margaret whispered a final goodbye to her mother.

"A wonderful adventure," she told her mother softly under her breath, for somehow she was sure her mother could hear.

"Soon we shall be together again, Margaret," she heard a voice reply inside her. "Soon you will reign with me."

Margaret was surprised. The words had come to her so

clearly, as if her mother were right next to her speaking. *Perhaps*, thought Margaret, *perhaps it was one of those things her mother had said to her during their meeting that she had forgotten*. Tucked away in the depths of her heart it had come out at just the right moment.

"We will be coming back to Joona soon, won't we, Laurel?" Margaret asked the swan just to be doubly sure.

"Yes," Laurel assured her. "Your greatest test still lies ahead of you, Margaret. Then you shall return."

"What test?" Margaret asked.

"You will know soon enough," Laurel told her gently. "But do not trouble yourself about that yet. Because of your efforts, Joona has been restored and all is accomplished as it should be."

Laurel spread his wings wide and took off, soaring up and around the Penance Room.

"Goodbye!" shouted the swans together over the swelling melody. They waved their wings and called to Laurel and the children as Laurel flew up through the opening in the ceiling and out of sight. They were in Sebastian's throne room now. Margaret could see the room clearly without all the sulfur haze. It was actually a lovely room with white pillars and a golden throne on a marble platform. The windows had been flung open and Laurel headed for one of them. They could see the rainbow through it, shining in full strength.

"This room is your mother's throne room, Margaret," Laurel called back to her. "She has opened the windows so the music can be heard and aired it out so that the aroma of pine and lilac can return."

They flew through the window into the blue sky that enveloped them in a welcoming fragrant breeze. The water beneath them was as clear as glass and the music danced at them, growing stronger as they approached the rainbow, which was soon upon them. They penetrated the brilliant green band of color first, then the crimson, the gold, and finally the purple. The music was strong and vibrant until they reached the end of the purple band. Here it became muddled and the notes ran into each other.

"Why can't earth learn how to play this music?" Ryan cried out. "It's too beautiful to leave behind!"

"I've never heard anything so glorious!" exclaimed Heather.

"Perhaps one day the world shall learn to play it," Laurel shouted back. "Until then you must play it in your hearts."

Then everything became dark. They were in the cave now with the sound of gurgling, rushing water, and the music was gone. For a moment the children were blinded and couldn't see. They were swaying back and forth as Laurel sped through the tunnel, whipping around the craggy turns and flapping powerfully just above the river.

"The water's high," Laurel told them. "Not as much room to fly. I'm going as fast as I can. Children, I must confess to you that we have lost an entire day on earth."

"It's Saturday?" Margaret gasped.

"Saturday morning," Laurel nodded.

The children looked at each other aghast. They had missed Friday completely. They were passing the waterfall now and the shimmering, quiet pool. The light flooding in from the ceiling made the waterfall multicolored like a rainbow.

"Well," Craig called up to Laurel, "you might as well turn around now and take me back. Otherwise I won't be alive to return next time. My dad will kill me."

Heather nodded her agreement.

"You underestimate your father's good intentions," Laurel said. "Peace, children."

They hurtled down through the cave. The walls were moist and dark, and the river was bursting with enthusiasm. Finally, in what seemed too short a time, they broke out of the cave into the gray dawn of morning. The birds were whistling groggy tunes and the air had a damp chill to it.

"I'm doomed, Laurel," Margaret said, nestling deeper into the bird's down to keep warm. "Uncle John is going to send me to hateful Auntie Emily. He said he would if I ever ran away again. Take us back, Laurel! Take us all back! I can't bear the thought of it—living in her apartment in the city. Her apartment smells of powder, Laurel, and it has all kinds of funny dark, curvy furniture with doilies on top. I shall run away."

"Gee whiz, my mother is going to ground me forever," Ryan said, his eyes bugging out. "She grounded me once for three whole months, but then she changed her mind after about a month and a half. She said I was under her feet too much and she wanted me to go outside. Said she hadn't intended to be punished along with me, but that's the way it was working out."

Laurel chuckled.

"Peace, children," he said again.

They flew back in between the mountains that were blue and misty and over the long ribbon of river that wound its way beneath them. After a while Laurel banked and flew over the Fitzgeralds' field.

"Hey!" yelled Craig. "Laurel! You're passing my house."

"Your parents are at Margaret's house," Laurel told them. "So is your mom, Ryan. They've been up all night waiting for you four. Don't worry, children. It will be all right."

They reached Margaret's house sooner than any of them wanted to. The light was on in the living room and there were people moving about inside. A patrol car was parked outside behind John's Jeep and two other vehicles. Margaret sighed and slowly climbed off Laurel's back. The others followed. Margaret's heart was in her throat.

"Laurel," she whispered. "What are we going to do?"

"Go in, Margaret," Laurel told her, and bent down low in

a swan smile. "Believe me when I tell you that all will be well. Give your uncle the stone."

The stone! Perhaps it would help matters, anyway. Margaret climbed the steps to the front door. Behind her, Ryan, Craig, and Heather followed. She was too scared to just barge in. Besides, it might shock everyone. Timidly, she rang the doorbell. There was a shuffling and flurry of movement. The door swung wide seconds later and she was staring into her uncle's lined, tired face.

"Margaret!" he cried.

She saw the tears leap to his eyes. Before she knew what was happening he swept her off her feet and she was caught up in his arms in a strong embrace.

The other parents were at the door now. She could hear Ryan's mother weeping, Craig's and Heather's mother sobbing and their father yelling. Uncle John put his hand on Casey's shoulder.

"C'mon, Casey," he said reassuringly. "They're okay, Casey."

Casey kept yelling.

"Blasted kids!" he roared. "I thought you two were dead! Dead and still as two nails in a fencepost!"

A police officer who had been standing in the corner of the room came forward looking relieved.

"Well folks," he said with a smile, "I'll call off the search. I must say, I'm glad to be on duty when there's a happy ending. It certainly made my day. I'll take their stories down at the station this afternoon. Right now, get them something to eat and take care of them."

"Wait!" Wilda called after him as the officer made his way toward the door. "We're still missing one. Ryan! Where's my Theodore?"

Wilda was shaking Ryan lightly, her face harried and frantic.

"Mom," Ryan said. "It's okay, Mom. He's on his way."

"On his way from where?" Wilda demanded.

"He's still in Joona, Mom," Ryan said, for he didn't know what else to say. "He'll be here."

"Are you sure he's coming, son?" the officer asked Ryan.

"I'm positive," Ryan assured the officer.

"Ma'am, if for any reason he doesn't show up in the next hour or two, we'll continue the search. But that Theodore, we've looked for him before. He's been known to wander and he always shows up on his own at some point. I'm not nearly as concerned about him as I was about these four. Theodore knows the area like a map."

"I know," Wilda said, her face relaxing a bit. "Theodore's been away at times much longer than this. I'll keep you posted, officer."

The policeman left. Casey half-shut, half-slammed the door behind him. Then the little group finally sat down. Beatrice Fitzgerald was a portly woman and took up most of the space on the love seat with Craig and Heather wedged in on either side of her. John and Wilda sat on the couch. Margaret nestled up on her uncle's lap and Ryan sat next to his mother. Wilda put her arm around Ryan's shoulders and squeezed him. Casey was the last to sit down. He was still fuming and yelling even though no one was paying attention. Finally, at Uncle John's suggestion, he managed to sit down on the wicker rocker.

"Where the blazes have you kids been?" Casey bellowed at Heather and Craig. "Do you have any sort of clue how worried your mother and I were? Good gosh! I thought you'd have more respect for us than just wandering off with no explanation, without even a thought as to what we must be going through. It's an insult to my training of you both. And you, Heather, missing a whole day of school! I can't remember when you last missed a day!"

He sounded like a locomotive blasting out steam.

"Calm down, Casey," Beatrice ordered. "Let the children speak without you breathing down their necks."

The children looked at each other, uncertain of what to say. Margaret cleared her throat and reached into her overall bib pocket. She handed the stone to Uncle John.

"This is from my mother," she told him and placed it in his hand. "She said it would remind you of when you were in Joona and help you to know that she is still alive. We've been with Laurel, Uncle John. In Joona. There was a takeover by the Regalia and Laurel wanted us there to help."

John stared at the stone in his hand as if it were pure gold.

"The white pearl rock! We built the platform for the throne and the pillars in the castle out of these when we were kids! Look, Wilda!"

John handed the rock to Ryan's mother.

"We had to dive for those rocks," he continued excitedly. "Off of the shore. They lay under the water like a shimmering treasure. Laurel needed landbred creatures to help with the work. Great Scott! I had forgotten all about this. At times I thought it was just a dream. Margaret, you mean you actually saw Annie?"

Margaret nodded.

"She's queen of the swans, Uncle John. And she's beautiful."

"She certainly is," echoed Heather. "She wears jewels in her hair."

"What is going on, John?" Wilda asked, looking completely confused, turning the rock about in her hands. "Who is Laurel?"

"Laurel!" Casey declared. "If this is more of that swan nonsense, I'll bash my brains in! C'mon, John! I thought you were a physician. You know, intelligent, scientific. A nuts and bolts kind of guy. What's gotten into you? This is kid's play! Nonsense!"

Casey got up from his rocking chair and planted himself over by the window, staring out of it like a bull ready to charge through. Margaret could see the veins in his neck sticking out and pulsating through his skin.

"Blasted kids!" he lashed out again. "With all the things a man's got to worry about, he shouldn't need to worry about the whereabouts of his children. And I have plenty else to worry about."

A subtle aroma had entered the room. Margaret noticed it at once and looked at Ryan, Heather, and Craig. They looked back knowingly, having recognized it also. At first it was only a light aroma, barely distinguishable from the usual smell of oak wood and dust that were characteristic of the living room. Now it was getting stronger, so strong that Wilda, an avid gardener, sat up suddenly.

"What's that fragrance?" she asked pointedly, looking at the children quizzically. "It smells like lilacs, but it can't be. It's not the season."

A breeze rushed in through the open window above the bookcase. Then the front door whipped open and a warm wind, rich with the fragrance of pine and lilac, came wafting in on them.

"Hey," said Casey, turning around suddenly. "I just slammed that door shut!"

"It is lilacs," Wilda said, the wind blowing her loose hair up around her face. "Lilacs and pine."

"And this is Laurel," Margaret announced, running over to the doorjamb, the other children excitedly following. "Isn't he beautiful?"

"Stop being impertinent," Casey declared. "There's nothing there. Now shut the blasted door."

"Of course there is, Dad," Heather exclaimed, a bit irritated at her father's continual outbursts. "Standing right there."

The swan was as obvious to the children as Casey's yelling had been moments before. There in the door stood Laurel. The wound in his chest was bold and bright and his wings were spread wide. He stood there like a statue, staring at them all with brilliant eyes that danced and flickered like diamonds in the sunlight.

John stood to his feet. He saw the swan also.

"Laurel!" he cried out. "Laurel, it's so good to see you. Thank you for keeping our children safe and . . . oh Laurel! Give Annie my love, and here," he added, fumbling around in his pocket for his key chain. "Here, give her this for me."

John was undoing something from his key ring that looked to Margaret like it might be a leather strap. What he actually produced once he got it off the key ring was a small leather pouch with a snap.

"What the devil is going on around here?" Casey demanded. "I've seen that blasted swan before and he's not there now. I'm telling you, John . . . if this is some kind of a joke, it's not a funny one."

"I don't see anything either, dear," Beatrice chimed in. "Just the front yard."

Wilda was silent. She just kept staring at the open door, squinting her eyes. John walked over to the door, ignoring Casey's rantings.

"Inside this pouch is Annie's impossibility ring," John continued. "You gave it to her, Laurel, the first time she went to Joona as a kid. The diamond was a weapon, remember? It blinded the enemy and then you healed them. She wore it up until the day she . . . the day she died, if you can call it that. I've saved it all these years and I thought she'd like to have it back."

Laurel closed his wings. He looked up at John with deep

affection. John handed Laurel the pouch and the swan reached out his neck for it and took it gently in his beak. The children stood for a moment stroking Laurel's soft white head. Laurel looked at each of them. The pouch was in his mouth so he didn't say anything, but the tender yearning in his eyes said far more than a simple farewell could ever express. He loved them. Then, quickly, almost as if he was forcing himself to leave, Laurel turned away. He opened his immense white wings, and with effortless ease took off toward the morning sky. He circled higher and higher into the misty morning stillness until he was just a tiny black fleck against the clouds. As he disappeared from their sight, Margaret heard the clear sound of trumpeting. She grabbed her uncle's hand.

"He's given us the victory call again!"

"Once again!" Uncle John repeated, a broad grin spreading across his face. He squeezed Margaret's hand tight.

"That means all is well."

"Did you see him, Mom?" Ryan asked Wilda eagerly, going over to his mother.

Wilda was still sitting on the couch squinting. She nodded slightly.

"Yes, Ryan," she said softly, visibly moved. "For a split second I think I saw him and then he faded away. He's enormous, and very white, isn't he?"

Ryan nodded.

"It's almost as though I remembered him from somewhere before, long ago."

"Honestly?" Casey asked. "You saw something, Wilda? Are you sure?"

Wilda nodded, tears coming to her eyes.

"I think I did. If only I could see him again. Just once more."

"I need a drink," Casey mumbled.

He grabbed a plaid jacket off the back of the couch and began to put it on.

"No drinking, Casey," Beatrice said firmly.

"But . . ." began Casey in protest. "I'm going to lose my mind here."

"Hardly," John countered. "Sit down."

Casey looked at his wife and then at Uncle John. Reluctantly he made his way over to the wicker rocker and sat down sheepishly.

"If you only had a mite of compassion for a penniless man," he pouted sullenly. "Maybe you'd all be a bit more kind."

"I haven't an ounce of compassion for you, Casey Fitzgerald, when you bring up booze," Beatrice exploded.

"Oh my!" Heather exclaimed. "I almost forgot! Here, Dad. Laurel found this for you."

She reached into the back pocket of her jeans and drew out Casey's wallet.

"It was downstream between two rocks. It must have fallen out of your pocket that night we went to the river."

She handed the wallet to her father. Casey's eyes grew as round as wagon wheels.

"Land sakes, girl!" he hooted.

He searched the wallet momentarily and drew out a stack of bills.

"My money!" he yelled. "My money! Here I was plumb broke and the next second I've got my money back. This was the advance on my crops, folks. Our eating money for the next six months."

He wagged the stack of bills in front of Heather's face.

"Girl, you have just saved this family from bankruptcy and shame."

Casey's face wore a wide grin.

"It wasn't me, Dad," Heather told him softly. "It was Laurel. He found it for you."

"That swan?"

Casey paused and looked searchingly into his daughter's face. Until now he hadn't realized how pretty she was becoming. She wasn't lying to him either. He could tell from the way her eyes met his in a steady blue gaze. He didn't understand about swans and magic lands. All he knew was that his daughter was convinced of something and that she meant he needed to believe her.

"Well, I'll be," Casey said finally.

He furrowed his brow and pursed his lips trying to understand. Then he just shook his head in amazement.

"Well, I'll be," he repeated. "If that just isn't the living end."

Margaret was still standing at the open door staring at the spot in the sky where Laurel had disappeared from view.

"Yes," she said softly. "That's exactly what it is. The living end."